Diva

Model Student Book Three

Model Student

DIVA IS THE third book of the *Model Student Series* by Devon Layne. The series comprises six books in nine volumes and is now available for order or pre-order. All beautifully designed and reasonably priced, Elder Road Books make an attractive addition to any connoisseur's collection.

And for those who look inside, the characters and storyline will captivate as much as Devon's sensitive and sensuous sex scenes. Here's what readers have said:

> *A six part longer story, the characters feel like real people*
> *even though they are in a pretty rare type of arrangement.*
> *They each struggle and fail and try again.*
> *Great long read with fantastic sex scenes throughout .*

> *An engaging and well-written story.*
> *But some of the writing, when describing Tony producing his*
> *masterpieces, is absolutely sublime.*

To order additional copies, see https://www.createspace.com/6529203. For more information and to inquire about dealer pricing contact Devon@DevonLayne.com.

Devon Layne

Diva

Model Student Book Three

ELDER ROAD BOOKS
BELLEVUE WA

One

WE WERE quite the crew at the Gala opening of PCAD's student exhibition. I'd walked in with two little boys and eight stunning women. We were head-turners, for sure, but we happened to stumble in just as art critic Bob Bowers was talking to a group about our paintings. It wasn't just about my painting. He pointed out the great interplay between it and Kate's charcoal.

When I looked at my eyes in Kate's drawing, I could see all the depression, the hope, the love, and the doubt I'd experienced this year. Standing where I was, I could even see her reflected in my eyes. Beneath the eyes were the shadowy shape of two fingers, pointing to them. "Look here," they seemed to say.

I might have stood there for an hour with an arm wrapped around Kate and the rest of our entourage near us if it hadn't been for the small voice that broke through the surrounding din.

"Mommy, I feel sick."

With four little words our evening went to hell. They were barely out of Damon's mouth before dinner followed them. Lissa bent to take care of him as I ran to the janitor's closet for cleanup supplies. Mop, bucket, rags, water, and some of that foul smelling cleanser that's guaranteed to make anyone sick who isn't already.

Allison managed to step out of the way of her "date" quickly enough to avoid getting anything on her. Lissa rushed Damon to the restroom and I got back to the exhibit in time to hear Drew say, "Meddy…" and then throw up in the opposite direction. Amy was not as lucky as Allison and found herself standing in a liquid lake. Melody carried Drew to the ladies' room as I flung rags onto the mess on the floor.

"Oh god, I feel…" Amy looked faint and Sonia slipped in beside her to prop her up. Before she walked away, I managed to lift each of her feet and thoroughly wipe her shoes and toes. Sonia motioned for Allison to help her and the trio moved out of the room rapidly. I looked around. Kate had gone with Melody, so my selection of assistants had instantly been reduced to Sandra and Bree.

Bree took one look, said, "Gah-ross!" and walked away. I was surprised to find Sandra down on her knees in her evening gown mopping up the rags and dumping them in a plastic bag. I grabbed the mop and started quickly cleaning the floor.

"Sandra, you don't have to do that. You're all dressed up. I can take care of it."

"I've got five little brothers and sisters," Sandra answered. "I'm used to cleaning up this kind of shit. We'll have it all taken care of in a few minutes."

About that time Jack arrived.

"You're a little over-dressed for janitorial work, Tony," he said.

"Jack! You just missed the excitement. Both boys just threw up." He went pale.

"Where are they? Are they all right?"

"Women's room with Lissa and Melody," I said. Jack was gone in a flash.

Sandra and I finished cleaning up the floor and put out a "Wet Floor/Piso Mojado" sign. I wheeled the cleanup supplies back to the closet. We didn't bother trying to rinse the rags, but just tied the garbage bag shut and I took it out back to the dumpster while Sandra held the door open so I wouldn't get locked out. The whole thing had only taken about ten minutes and we headed for the restroom.

Crying boys, girls in formals, two guys in tuxes. You get the idea. It was chaos. The poor little guys were bad and getting worse.

"Jack, we need to get them to the doctor. Damon is burning up with a fever. How could I have missed him getting sick?"

"Both of them," Jack said. "We should head to Children's."

"We've got the limo outside. We can take you," I offered. Damon had grabbed one of my hands as soon as I walked through the door. Jack was holding Drew, but the younger boy hadn't let go of Melody.

"We'll take my car," Jack said. "That way you aren't stranded."

"It's okay. Melody and I will come with you," I argued. Jack turned to me.

"Listen, Tony. I appreciate your help and Melody's quick actions, too. But it's a big night for you and you shouldn't leave the party before it's even started."

"But…"

"Tony," Jack spoke sharply, "these are Lissa's and my kids. It's our responsibility, not yours." I stepped back, about ready to blast him. How dare he insinuate that I didn't care? Lissa was my girlfriend, not his wife.

"Sweetheart," Lissa said, "Jack's right. I know how much you and Melody love Damon and Drew, but this is something their parents need to take care of and you should be out with your friends. Don't forget, you're leaving Sunday and everyone will be gone for the summer long before you get back. Help us get the boys to the car and then come back and enjoy yourselves. I'll let you know as soon as we find out what's going on."

I bit back my response. Lissa didn't need another little boy to distract her. She needed a man. Her husband. I picked up Damon in my arms and carried him to the car. Melody extracted the promise that they'd call as soon as they knew what was going on.

MELODY AND I walked back into the gallery. Other than the yellow sign on the floor and a lingering smell of disinfectant, the party was going on as normal. I caught a glimpse of Bob Bowers entertaining his group in front of the mural and supposed that Jack was right. I should introduce myself. We spotted our remaining dates in a corner by the punch bowl, listening avidly to Allison.

"My god! They kept me awake half the night listening and the other half imagining what had been going on!" she said to the girls' laughter. "You should have heard him!"

"Oh they were probably just putting on a show for you," Bree said caustically. "All fake."

"Hey, I've had some experience with 'fake,'" Allison responded. "I'd have known if it was fake. Let me tell you, if I could do that to a man, I'd charge rent."

"Oh," Kate moaned. "I wish I could inspire passion like that." I looked at Melody and we both nearly choked. *If only Kate knew!* We made some noise and walked up to the group.

"Hey guys. Had enough excitement for the evening?" I asked casually. At least three of the girls blushed.

"Exciting is still to come, baby. I like art, but enough is enough, already," Bree said. "Let's go party!" She was starting to get on my nerves. What the hell was wrong with her? She raised her arms in the air and started to wiggle her hips in what I assumed was supposed to be a dance move.

"Tony, Melody, I'd like you to meet my boyfriend," Sonia said. "This is Thor. Thor, I've told you about Melody and Tony."

"Oh yeah," he said. "You sure have. It's nice to meet you. And I just want to say thank you for Sunday night." Sonia blushed a very pretty crimson beneath her blonde hair and playfully punched her boyfriend on the arm. Thor. What an appropriate name. He looked like a Scandinavian god. He was a six-four, 230-pound blond—built like a rock. Thor and Sonia together looked like wet dreams for both men and women.

"Nice to meet you, Thor," I said, letting him crush my hand in his. "What do you play?"

"Bassoon," he replied. I looked at him quizzically. "Yeah," he continued. "Everybody figures I'm some kind of football player. I march in the band. I'm a music education major."

"No kidding?" Melody said. "Welcome to PCAD."

"I'm not that good," Thor said. "I like to play, but I really want to teach."

"If people like you didn't teach, kids like us would never go into the arts," I said. "Speaking of which, I don't suppose I could get you two to pose for me, could I? I don't mean any-thing… you know… I mean kind of a classic composition… if you aren't opposed to doing something nude."

"You've already done her," he laughed. Sonia wasn't getting any relief from the blush that colored her. I wondered if I could capture that with paint. "Adding me shouldn't take much," Thor continued. *Except in the amount of paint,* I thought. "Hey, I tell you what. If you can get me an invite to the next posing party like the one I heard about Sunday night, I'll pose any way you want me to. I got a blow-by-blow description, so to speak, after Sonia got home Sunday night."

"I think that might be arranged," I said. "It would probably make the night a little easier on me."

"Yeah. I can imagine how hard it could get."

We laughed. I know—but no matter how old it is, male erectile humor is always funny. I turned to the rest of the group and singled out Kate.

"Ms. Holsinger, may I ask you to accompany me? There is someone I've been told we should meet," I said. Well, Jack had said *I* should meet Bob Bowers, but after I heard what he said about Kate's charcoal, I realized she should meet him, too.

Kate took my arm and we walked out to the mural hallway where the art critic was working his way down the various focal points in the mural. She had one hand beneath my elbow, but as we waited politely for a break, her other hand softly stroked up and down my bicep. When Mr. Bowers came to a break and people started to move on, Kate and I stepped forward.

"Excuse me, Mr. Bowers. May I introduce Ms. Kate Holsinger? She is the artist who did the charcoal portrait you were admiring earlier," I said.

"Ah, Ms. Holsinger. I'm so pleased to meet such a great talent. Do you have other pieces on display?"

"A few, Mr. Bowers. Nothing I like as much as the portrait. Your review this morning was very kind." I'd forgotten all about the review. In fact, I never got around to reading it.

"Well, please give me a tour," he said. Then he turned to me. He looked into my eyes and held them. "And I assume you're Tony Ames."

"Uh… yes, sir. Pleased to meet you. How did you know?"

"You are in each other's eyes, just as I could see you in Miss Grant's eyes in your mural painting. I hope you weren't disappointed in what I said in the review this morning."

"I guess I didn't read it," I answered. "Sorry."

"Good! Never put stock in what critics say anyway. We're paid to criticize."

"We learn from criticism," I said. "But please, I know you've spent plenty of time on my works, and I do appreciate the letter of recommendation Jack passed on to me. Please let Kate show you her other pieces. She's got a pretty amazing talent." Kate beamed at me. *Damn, she looked good in her evening gown.* She was wearing the orchid I'd given her last week, apparently kept fresh in the dormitory refrigerator. She was keeping a tight grip on my arm.

Mr. Bowers leaned in to speak to me in a whisper, intentionally blocking Kate from hearing.

"Tell me, Tony. Do you make love to all your models?" *What the fuck?* Did he just say what I thought he said? I calmed myself before I answered. It was obviously rhetorical.

"Only on canvas, sir."

Two

WE LEFT the gala a little after nine and the limo drove us to an over-eighteen club near the University of Washington. The music was good with a popular local DJ spinning the tunes. No alcohol was served so the club could handle underage partiers. All the way there, Melody and I were trying to reach Lissa to see how the kids were doing and if we were needed. I was pretty much ready to ditch everyone and just catch a cab to the hospital. It was driving me crazy, not knowing what was going on.

"Maybe we should just go over there," I said to Melody. "God, I hate not knowing how Damon and Drew are or what's wrong. Why did they have to take them to the emergency room?"

"Oh, lighten up, Tony," Bree broke in. "We're supposed to be partying. They're not your kids, after all."

"You're really a bitch, you know, Bree?" I shot back at her. "I'm not interested in listening to you put down the people I love. Shape up your attitude or go home."

"Listen, you little prick. I've been playing the game and waiting my turn. If you're not interested in me, maybe I should tell the athletic director a little more about your lifestyle and parties. I'm sure he'll be interested in the new talent's ability to represent SCU."

"Listen to yourself, Bree! Jesus. The man is your father. He's the athletic director, not your pimp." That earned me a slap across the face, and it stung.

"Bree!" Sonia yelled. She grabbed her friend by the arm and dragged her away from me mouthing something at me over her head that I couldn't understand. At least she was gone. My face hurt.

"Really, Dude?" Thor said to me. *Shit.* Was he going to get on my case now, too? "That was awesome. Somebody's needed to take her down a peg for a long time. Welcome to SCU."

"Thanks, I think," I said. Melody reached up and kissed my cheek.

"I'm not doing anything tonight to ruin our night with friends," Melody whispered. "But next time I'm alone with her, I'm going to kick her freckled ass into the next county."

"I'm not justifying her or anything," Thor said, "but I think she might be on something. She's not acting normal, even for Bree. She's a pushy slut, but she's not usually that crass. Something must have set her off."

"She's just realized what different worlds we live in," Amy offered. "Aside from her being hot for Tony, we're probably as much to blame as her about polarizing things. She's an athlete and we're artists. This was the first time she saw what Tony's art world really looks like. Sunday it was just a guy partying with a bunch of naked girls. She's trying to get him back there."

"Wow! Are you studying psychology, Amy?" I laughed. It was good to have friends around me, especially when I was feeling bad about causing a scene. I knew she didn't mean anything.

"You need to add a 'u-s' in that word and then you've got it right." I *wasn't* getting it and looked at her strangely, I guess.

"*Pussy*chology," Amy laughed. "I'm making a career of analyzing as many of them as I can."

We all laughed and I was thankful that Amy was there and that we were mostly all friends. We were finally at the head of the line to get in and Sonia and Bree returned to stand opposite Thor from us. Bree refused to look in our direction, but her mascara had run and there was a black streak on her cheek. I gave Melody a squeeze, took a deep breath, and walked over to Bree.

"I'm sorry I snapped at you, Bree," I said. "I can't blame you for not understanding a weird situation." I reached up with my handkerchief and wiped the smudge off her face. She looked at me and her lower lip started to quiver, but she kept the tears back. "Friends?"

"Thank you," she said softly. She reached up and patted my cheek where she'd hit me. "Sorry I can't wipe that off."

Well, that was as good as it was going to get for tonight. We got into the club, got sodas, and danced. I could see that we weren't really an integrated group any more. Amy joined Bree, Sonia, and Thor on the dance floor and the four seemed to trade partners regularly if partners were called for. Most of the time, it was just everyone dancing together. Amy was working hard at comforting Bree. Hmmm. Was Sonia intentionally trying to get between them?

Melody, Allison, Kate, and Sandra were with me. Kate looked like she was in heaven when she was dancing with Melody or with me. In fact, neither Melody nor I missed exactly how heavenly she looked. There might have been just a little more touching and brushing against each other than the dances called for. But she looked like she was *near* heaven even when she danced with Sandra and Allison. It was nice to see her having fun.

Melody and I checked our phones every few minutes for messages. Between the pounding bass of the music and the crowd noise in the room, it would be impossible to either hear our phones or feel them vibrate. At midnight, we called an end to our little prom and asked our limo driver to take us the long way home, whatever that was. We had an hour left on the rental and were determined to use it all.

--------⊲♦⊳--------

IT WAS BITTERSWEET. My freshman year was over. Classmates that I'd met just nine months ago were now my lover and friends. I had another lover sitting with her ex-husband and two kids in a hospital. A cute student from Kansas had become a close friend. Two cheerleaders and a Norse god were friends from a new school. It was hard to remember why I'd been so depressed just a few weeks ago.

Sonia would be returning home to LA. Her plan was to spend the summer in the surf as she had done for the past several years. Thor was planning to visit his parents and then join Sonia. We were, of course, all invited to come down to visit.

Bree was staying put. She'd sobered up and was quiet in the car, but said she usually helped her dad during the summer when he went out to recruit athletes who had not yet committed. Most of it would be in the Northwest because SCU simply wasn't big enough to draw athletes from further away. Being a Division III school wasn't much to brag about, but the program was growing and she was determined to do her part.

"And no, I don't recruit athletes by fucking them," Bree said. "We just talk and, if they come to visit, then they know someone who will show them around. I'm not always a slut." Melody was still pretty pissed at her, but even she tried to be enthusiastic about Bree's job.

"I'm going back across the mountains after next weekend to fend off the breeders for the summer. I'll be... oh god, you just wouldn't believe what I do in the summer," Amy said.

"Come on, Amy," I encouraged. "Fess up. I bet you paint houses."

"That would be a great job!" Amy said enthusiastically. "Especially compared to what I really do." She waited for us to egg her on a little more and then continued. "All right, I live in a resort community in the mountains. Everything has a Bavarian theme. I mean everything. At the local drive-in, you can order schnitzel. I know, because I work there."

"Do you cook or wait tables?" Sandra asked.

"God, this is so embarrassing. It's a drive-in. An old fashioned one. I dress in a cute little Bavarian maiden outfit and roller skate to people's cars to take their orders. When things are slow, we do trick skating in the parking lot. That usually brings people in."

"Wait. You do roller skating tricks in a little Swiss Miss costume for the summer?" Melody howled. "You know if you'd have pulled that on me last fall you might have gotten lucky!"

"Well, it's never too late to try. You know, Tony, just because I won't do you doesn't mean we couldn't double-team the little brat," Amy said.

"I don't know, Amy," I said. "The very thought of you in that little short skirt and skates just makes me want to yodel."

When asked, Sandra said that she was going to spend her summer being the chauffeur to her five little brothers and sisters and try to give her mother a break. She was the oldest by five years, then the rest all came fast and furious. All five were between 10 and 14 years old with one set of twins.

Allison would go with Lissa and me to Chicago Sunday night and watch National Singles and then head back to Kansas for her summer job as entertainment director at a YMCA camp.

"Kate, where will you spend the summer?" Melody asked.

"Oh, I'll be around. I've got a job as a docent at the Art Museum. Mostly, I'll be giving groups of kids, about Damon's age, tours of the children's collection. I think it'll be fun," Kate said. "Or I'll be dead. I'm not sure which."

"Okay. What about you guys?" Sonia asked. "Planning a summer full of art and naked slumber parties?"

"You guys all have the wrong idea," Melody said. "We really aren't that wild."

"We were there, you know," Allison said.

"And exactly how big an orgy did we have?" I asked.

"Well, we didn't actually *do* anything," Kate agreed. "But that doesn't mean we weren't *thinking* about it."

"Kate!" Sandra exclaimed. "My, the girl has come out of her shell!"

"I'm flying out to Chicago to join Allison, Lissa and Tony as soon as my last final is done on Thursday," Melody said. "Then I'll sit with Saul and Deborah and my parents to watch my boyfriend win a national championship. I can't wait to meet them in person, Tony. And it will be so weird to have my parents meeting your parents."

"We'll spend the weekend in Chicago," I continued. "Then Melody has to go home to Boston for a while and Lissa will have to get back here to work and take care of the boys. I'll go back to Nebraska for a while and then I'm coming back out here so I can start helping Lissa get ready for Opens. As soon as Melody gets back we'll all be together again."

The limo pulled up in front of Bree's house and the three SCU students got out. Well, we all got out, because you can't just say goodbye without hugs and kisses. Bree's kiss was a little tentative and less aggressive, but she did hug me pretty fiercely. She hugged Melody, too, and said something to her that I couldn't hear. I glanced at Thor in time to see Amy go into a lip lock with him, so I used that opportunity to plant a good one on Sonia. She giggled.

"I hope you'll be seeing more of us in the fall," she said, and laughed as she got swept up in an even more passionate kiss by Amy.

We piled back into the limo and took the next three back to the dorm. Sandra came at me for a big open-mouthed kiss, but I stopped her and used my fingers to close her mouth.

"Kissing is about the lips," I said as I leaned in and caressed her lips with mine, then brushed my tongue against them. I gave her a squeeze and backed away. She didn't move, but just stayed there with her face upturned and a look of bliss. Melody used the opportunity to kiss her just as sweetly. We could see her chest heaving in deep breaths and her huge nipples straining at the fabric of her gown, bra be damned.

"Why didn't anybody ever tell me that before," she said dreamily.

Allison hugged her new friends and I hugged Amy and gave her a little kiss that she accepted as one good friend to another. Melody wasn't so demure, however. She gave Amy the works.

"Holy shit," Amy gasped. "What finally came over you?"

"I just had this image of you on skates in that little skirt and peasant blouse," Melody laughed. "It was just so hot."

Melody and I stood in front of Kate while Allison was hugging Sandra and Amy and suggesting that they come to Kansas for a visit. We closed in on her at the same time and kissed her cheeks. Kate smiled and turned to Melody. She kissed her tenderly, then turned to me and did the same thing. She sighed.

"I wish Lissa were here," she said softly. "That would be just right. I hope I'll see you guys later this summer. Call me?"

"Oh yeah," Melody said. "This is from Lissa." We both moved in on Kate with what had become practiced precision in three-way kissing. Kate could hardly kiss us back, she was grinning so hard.

"Wow! That girl can really kiss, can't she?" Kate giggled.

We promised we would call her as soon as we were back in town. Everyone verified that we had everyone else's phone numbers in our contacts and the last three of us returned to the limo.

I sat between Melody and Allison and they snuggled up to me on either side. It was pleasant having the two there, but it just wasn't… right. Allison was sweet, but she wasn't Lissa.

Three

MELODY'S PHONE rang at 1:01 a.m., just after we'd walked into the house. We were headed to the boys' room to see if everyone was there. No one was, but Lissa greeted Melody on the phone and asked her to put it on speaker so she could talk to both of us.

"We're still at the hospital, but will probably be leaving soon," Lissa started. She sounded drained.

"How are they? What's wrong?" Melody asked.

"We've been worried all night," I added.

"It turns out there's a nasty bug that's hit in past couple of days and is spreading like crazy through the pre-school and elementary schools. We must have seen a dozen people we knew in the emergency room. It's crazy here. Their temperatures peaked at 104 degrees and the doctors pumped them full of antibiotics, but it will be at least a couple of days before they are fully healthy," Lissa said.

"When will you be home? Should we come and get you?" I asked.

"I'm not coming back tonight," Lissa said. Melody and I looked at each other and I could see worry creasing her brow.

"Lissa?"

"We're taking the boys to Jack's house. I can't bring them home with all of you there. The doctors say it's really contagious.

You can't risk being sick the last week of school and at National Singles. We'll be lucky if you haven't already caught it," Lissa explained. It was logical but we weren't happy.

"But Jack's there. You could come home," Melody pled.

"Sweetheart, I can't leave my boys tonight. They won't let go of me and I wouldn't leave them when they're sick anyway. I'll stay there."

"With Jack?" I blurted out before I could stop my mouth. I was worried sick about the boys, and I understood that Lissa needed to be with them, but she'd be there with the boys *and with Jack*. It was like they were still married.

"It's not about Jack, Tony," Lissa said sharply. "I can't expect you two to understand, but please just accept that I need to be here. I'll talk to you tomorrow."

Melody recovered first and managed to stop Lissa before she hung up.

"We love you, Lissa. And we love Damon and Drew. Give them a hug for us and tell them we love them. Please?"

"We love you, too, Little One. I'm sorry I snapped at you, Tony. It's been a hard night. I love you both."

AFTER A LITTLE peck on the lips, Allison had gone straight to the guest room and Melody and I retired to our bed. Our bed—but Lissa's bed. It felt so strange to get ready and crawl into Lissa's bed without Lissa in it. Even when Melody came into my arms, she seemed hesitant and unsure.

It wasn't like we hadn't made love without Lissa, nor that Lissa hadn't made love with each of us without the other. But it was strange being in *this* bed without her. Even with two of us sharing it, it felt big and empty.

"Tony?" Melody said in a very small voice.

"What is it, Meddy?"

"I'm afraid." I didn't need an explanation but we both needed to give it voice. I could feel the fear gnawing at me.

"So am I, dear."

"Are you afraid Lissa won't come back to us?"

"Yes. Afraid that she is sharing this crisis with Jack instead of us and that anytime Damon and Drew are involved, she'll be with Jack. Afraid that we aren't as important to her as we want to believe." *Afraid that she was with him right now.* No, I didn't imagine that they were having sex while Damon and Drew ran a fever in the next room. Just that he was the one holding her and comforting her while she watched over her babies. I was afraid we could never compete.

"I keep thinking of how she tried to break up with us and we wouldn't let her. Are we clinging to a fantasy?"

"No, sweetheart. That can't be. What we have is real for all three of us. We just need to be patient and show her how much we love her."

"Tony, would we…would we…still be together without Lissa?" Tears were flooding down Melody's cheeks and I held and rocked her trying to ward off the dark clouds that threatened to engulf me. I couldn't answer. I held her fiercely and kissed the tears escaping from her eyes. I found her lips and we devoured each other—not hungrily, but desperately—hanging on to what was real in the face of what was imagined.

I wasn't quite hard and she wasn't quite wet, but we forced ourselves together, needing to be joined. As we rocked back and forth, our bodies took control and we slid more freely, my hardness penetrating deeply. I rolled her on top of me so

I wouldn't crush her and held her to me tightly. Our climax came, as the poet said, not with a bang, but a whimper.

———⊲◆⊳———

"YOU GUYS ARE sure a lot quieter when there's only two of you," Allison said when we appeared in the kitchen Saturday morning. She'd already made coffee and was staring at a bowl of cereal when we finally pushed ourselves out of bed. Neither of us wanted to get up, but we couldn't bear to stay in the bed any longer. Allison looked at us long and hard as I poured two cups of coffee and got out the milk and sugar for Melody.

"Oh, you poor kids," she said after a minute. She came around the table and pulled both of us to her and squeezed. We no longer had tears to shed. We were too exhausted. We both just rested our heads against Allison's ample bosom. "You are really in love with her, aren't you! And the boys. I saw it the last couple of days, but now it's written all over your faces. Don't worry; it will be okay. You'll see."

It was funny, being comforted like little kids by a woman who was only a couple years older than we were. This was going to be a long hard day if we didn't snap out of it. Hey, the boys would start getting well and then Lissa would come home and we'd all be fine again, right? I smooched Melody while Allison kept hold of our shoulders. She smiled a little and her eyes shifted up toward our comforter. I grinned and, as if on cue, we both turned our heads toward Allison and nipped at her nipples, prominently standing out in unfettered glory under her t-shirt. She yelped.

"You guys! I almost wet my pants! You scared me."

"Oh," I said. "Sorry about that. Next time we suck on your nipples we'll try not to startle you."

"Next time? Oh, shit!"

"Sorry we're so sour this morning," Melody said. "Thanks for helping us and giving us a hug."

"You're welcome," Allison said, starting to breathe again.

"But, yeah. Next time," Melody finished. Allison rolled her eyes.

"My god, what did I get myself into? Just come out to play some racquetball for a week. We'll have a couple of parties. So sure, I thought to myself. Sounds like fun. I wonder why they didn't tell me I'd be running around in a house full of naked women, listening to the most incredible sex I've ever imagined, and getting my boobs bitten by not just a boy, but a girl, too! Why didn't they mention these little details before I got here?"

"Oh, Allison," Melody complained. "If we'd told you all that it would have spoiled the surprise and you might not have come."

"Oh I think I'd have come… several times. I just might have packed lighter."

We all got a chuckle out of that and began the process of pulling ourselves out of the morose depths and back into daylight. We had work to do. Lissa, Allison, and I would be leaving for Chicago on Sunday. I wouldn't be back until summer, so I needed to clean out my dorm room. We wanted to rush over to Jack's house and visit the boys, but we knew they'd all had a hard night, so we decided to wait until later in the day. We didn't want to disturb desperately needed sleep, so moving out of the dorm was the first order of business after breakfast.

It wasn't that big a job to move because most of my stuff was already at Lissa's. Melody and I found some comfort in the fact that we were moving things to Lissa's house and Melody decided that she was going to move the rest of her things at the same time. That was more challenging because she still had things in my dorm room and in her original dorm room, as well as what she'd already moved to Lissa's.

Sandra came to help us gather things from Melody's dorm room and load them into Lissa's SUV. She said that Kate had convinced Amy to take her roller skating around Green Lake and show her Amy's dance moves. We decided that when we were all loaded we'd cruise by that direction and see if we could spot them.

We didn't see them and finally Allison, Melody and I got things back to Lissa's house and took all our crap downstairs.

"Geez, you guys have a lot of stuff for living in a dormitory. I forgot what it was like to have to move out in the spring."

"Where do you live now?" I asked.

"I rent a two-bedroom apartment with three other girls. It might as well be a dormitory with two single beds in each room and no weekday overnight guests allowed. The only good thing is it has two baths—or I guess they call it one-and-three-quarters. There's only a shower and no tub in the *en suite*. But I've got good roommates and the gal I share my bedroom with has a boyfriend with an apartment, so most weekends she's at his place and I have my own room."

It was fun to hear more about Allison's life at KSU.

"You don't have to move out in the summer?" I asked.

"No. We just re-upped our lease so we don't have to move out until after we graduate. It's a real relief to have a permanent home instead of temporary housing."

Melody and I looked at each other. It was the big question on both our minds. Were we moving into permanent housing?

Lissa, Melody, and I had talked about it a lot. We all three said we wanted to live together, but we had our family obligations, as well. After the tournament, I'd be headed to Nebraska to spend time with my parents and reconnect with old friends. Melody's mother and father planned to meet her in Chicago next weekend and spend a day with my folks before they went back to Boston. Lissa, of course, had a job and two kids. She'd be coming home from Chicago and we'd be in three different parts of the country for the first time.

We had agreed that Melody's and my things would stay at Lissa's house until we got back and then we would decide on permanent living arrangements. I just hoped I wasn't moving back to the dorms.

"MAYBE I SHOULD stay in the car," Allison said when we pulled up in front of Jack's house. It was located close enough to Lissa's place that they were in the same school district, but in vastly different neighborhoods. Jack lived in a small, older home that looked like it was out of a 1950s TV show, complete with a big front porch and storm door. We grabbed Allison's hand and dragged her along with us as we approached the door.

We knocked and waited. Finally, Jack opened the door. He looked terrible. He held up one finger in a wait-a-minute gesture and lowered the glass pane on the storm door so he could talk to us through the screen.

"I'm sorry, guys, but you can't come in. Lissa's orders. This bug is really bad and she doesn't want you exposed to it."

"Is everyone all right?" Melody asked. Well, of course not, if what Jack was saying was true.

"It's pretty bad," Jack said. "Neither of us have had much sleep. One or the other of the boys has been up all the time."

"What can we do to help?" I asked. "Can we see Lissa?"

"Lissa will come out as soon as she can. Are you guys willing to run an errand for us? We could use some groceries. I wasn't prepared for a siege and I don't think I should go out if I can help it."

"Of course!" I said. At last, I felt like we could *do* something! I really didn't care what. Jack hadn't unlocked the storm door, so there was no way I could even sneak in. He left and came back a few minutes later with a list and a hundred-dollar bill.

"Lissa's in the shower with Drew," Jack said when he got back. "Having the steam helps keep his nose and lungs open. She said she'll come out when you get back with the groceries. There's also a new prescription that the boys' pediatrician called in to Walgreen's. Here's my insurance card. It should cover the costs, but if anything costs more than what I've given you, just tell me."

"We'll be back soon," Melody said.

"You guys are real friends," Jack said warmly. "I know you want to be with Lissa and the boys, but Lissa is adamant about not exposing you if we can help it."

We went to the grocery store and picked up several cans of chicken soup, especially the kind with little letters in it that the boys like so much. Milk, juice, cereal… with three of us shopping, we were in and out of the store in fifteen minutes. It was a longer wait at the pharmacy. I couldn't believe the line of worn and tired looking parents who were standing in line for prescriptions and there were even a couple of whiny, sniffling kids being towed along. Melody insisted that Allison and I go back to the car because we had to travel the next day. Melody said that if she got sick it would have less impact.

"Maybe I could move in with Jack, too," she joked. It wasn't funny.

When we got the medicine and groceries back to Jack's house, Lissa answered the door and took the bags from us, but didn't allow us in. I touched her hand lightly when she took the bags and when she came back from the kitchen she brought a bottle of hand sanitizer and insisted that I use it immediately. She squirted some on each of us and then closed the door again quickly.

"I miss you," Lissa said, looking at Melody and me. "Sorry to expose you to all this mush, Allison. I'll get more hand sanitizer if it's too much." We all laughed a little. It was so good to be back with Lissa, even on opposite sides of the storm door.

"Well, at least we'll all be back together tomorrow," I said. "Do you want us to pack for you?"

"About that, Tony," Lissa said, looking down at her feet. "I'm not going to Chicago with you."

Four

OF COURSE it all made sense. Logical. Not to mention, the only thing we *could* do. Not only were Lissa's kids sick, she was coming down with it, too. She simply wouldn't—or couldn't—travel.

I decided on the spot that I wouldn't go either but the heated argument that ensued left me at three to one against my canceling the trip. Lissa said she would send instructions to Allison on coaching me through my first round. Sam would be headed out on Tuesday, but there was no way he'd make the early matches and it was pretty much guaranteed I'd be playing in one of the first two flights. Pairings would be announced Monday morning.

"So how would you like to be Ice Queen for a day?" Lissa asked Allison. "I'm depending on you to make sure Tony settles in, gets to the right places at the right time, and wins his matches, got it?"

"You're really going to risk sending your boyfriend across the country with me?" Allison said. Lissa looked at me and smiled, then looked at Allison.

"Tony knows what to do," she said simply. "Right, Melody?" Melody smiled and nodded.

"Oh, he sure does!"

———◁◆▷———

IT WAS A four-hour flight and we lost two hours crossing time zones, so it was already after eight in the evening when we landed. With the baggage fuck-ups and waiting for a taxi on Sunday night, it was ten by the time we got to the hotel downtown and got checked in.

It was all of five minutes later when I realized Allison and I were staying in the same room.

The room had two queen beds in it. When Lissa originally made our reservation, she decided to keep costs down and share one room. Rooms cost a lot more in Chicago than in Tempe.

But that arrangement was made when Lissa was going to be with us. Now it was just Allison and me.

———◁◆▷———

WE WENT ABOUT our nighttime routines, taking turns in the bathroom. I was nervous. I didn't know what to expect from Allison and I still wasn't sure I wanted anything to happen between us, even though both Lissa and Melody assured me that they expected something to happen and to enjoy myself. I was in a three-way text session with my girlfriends when Allison came out of the bathroom in a short terrycloth robe, drying her dark hair.

My lovers wished me goodnight and pleasant dreams, complete with a few giggles. I set my phone aside and turned in the bed I'd labeled 'mine'. Allison was still standing between the beds in the robe. Her bed had not been turned down yet.

"Uh… Allison," I began. "I don't want you to get the wrong impression. I really like you and all, but…"

"Exactly what would the right impression be?"

"That we're just a couple of friends sharing a room, right?"

"Yes, we're just a couple sharing a room," she teased.

"Allison, it's not…"

"Shut up, Tony." That brought my eyes up to focus on hers. She held me with a serious look and then, to my amazement and fear, she unfastened her robe and let it fall to the floor.

I can't deny my body's reaction to the sight not three feet in front of me. I was too close to take in all of her at one time, but as the robe fell, so did my eyes. Like Lissa, Allison is muscled and toned. She's an athlete. Her breasts are bigger than Lissa's. Hell, I think they are bigger than any of the girls' I'd seen over the past few weeks except Sandra. She has small dark areolae that are high enough on the curve of her breast that the hard nipples almost point toward the ceiling. Beneath these perfect mounds is a flat stomach and deeply indented navel. The swell of her hips and the rise of her mound are a counterpoint to the shape of her bosom. Her landing strip is as precise and neat as the rest of her body, her labia smooth and glistening.

As I looked at her, she slowly turned around, modeling her backside as calmly as if she were a manikin in a store window. Beautiful as her front was, her back was where her real power showed—maybe because there were fewer distractions. She had great muscle definition in her shoulders and back and she flexed her glutes to show that if her butt wiggled, it was definitely on purpose and not the result of uncontrolled fat. I could trace with my eyes the line of muscles I'd drawn in my first sketch of her as she raised on her toes and the muscles in her legs shifted beneath her pale skin. She continued her rotation until she was facing me again.

"So, Tony," she said casually, "do you see *anything* you haven't seen before?"

Well, I'd noticed a small mole just below her left ass-cheek, but I was pretty sure she was referring to the fact that she'd been naked in front of me twice before—once for most of a day. I was working my mouth, but words weren't coming out.

"Look, guy, I'm here as a substitute for Lissa. I'm going to do my best for you like Lissa does. I may not be her, but I'll still do whatever is necessary. Now, as your coach, exactly how much sex do you normally have before a competition?"

I thought back to Tempe, the only competition I'd been in since I started having sex at all. Lissa had been firm in not having sex before the match. I had my defense.

"I never have sex before a match," I said with relief.

"And that is exactly how much you can expect to have tonight," Allison said firmly. She reached behind her and took her t-shirt off the bed. She slipped it over her head and pulled it down. It only reached her waist. Yes, her magnificent tits were covered, but that landing strip was like an arrow pointing to the Promised Land.

"Tony."

"Huh?"

"You're still staring at my pussy."

Well, Christ, Allison! It's right at eye level. If it was any closer, I'd need reading glasses. What do you expect? Okay. I needed to get myself in focus and lighten up a bit.

"Oh yeah. Well, you see, Melody's always talking about you being a girl with real balls and I was just checking to see if I'd missed something." We laughed and the tension left the room. What a relief! She turned toward her bed and pulled the covers down, bending so that I had an absolutely clear view from the other side.

"Well?" she asked as she crawled into her bed. "Find anything?"

"No… but… don't you wear panties or something to bed?" She finally pulled the covers up and my eyes started to settle back into my head.

"Naw. After having been exceptionally naughty and wantonly displaying all my womanly charms to a horny guy a few feet away from me, I might need emergency access before I can get to sleep," she said, turning out the light. "'Night!"

That definitely wasn't meant to make my night more relaxing. In fact, I ended up soothing myself quietly in the bed across from her, imagining exactly what kind of emergency she might be experiencing as I came in my shorts.

Five

IN THE morning, Allison was all business, and she proved herself an efficient coach/manager. We were up early and headed for United Center where the Bulls play basketball and the Blackhawks play hockey. They bring in big boxes to set up each racquetball court complete with floor and ceiling. The one at center court was Plexiglass so spectators could sit around on three sides. The end wall was solid. With the seating pulled back to the hockey boundaries, there was room to set up twelve courts, plus an open area in the middle for the glass box. Tempe was great, but this was massive and unbelievable. Only half the courts were fully set and operational when we got there at half past eight and they were already full with athletes who were there early.

Registration went smoothly as far as I was concerned. Allison just told the person at the desk that Coach Grant was sick and she'd been sent by SCU to fill in for her. Since racquetball is a club sport and not an official NCAA sport, there's no clear demarcation about who is and isn't qualified to be a coach. I could have brought Mr. Miyagi. In addition to the rigidly set times on the official courts, six local athletic clubs had facilities available for practice and even some matches. With more than 350 competitors in town, court time was at a premium. The practice schedule was already set and we discovered my court reservation was not only at a club miles away, it was twenty minutes ago.

Then I saw Allison go into action.

"This is not acceptable. You can't assign a practice session before registration opens in the morning."

"All the athletes currently on the courts had practice before registration opened. We just got them in and they register afterward."

"And how did they know to be here at that time?"

"They were all notified."

"Tony Ames was not notified."

"We sent the information to his coach."

"His coach is ill."

"Not our problem."

"Do you know who his coach is?" That stopped the conversation. The registration person shuffled through the papers.

"Someone named Lissa Grant," the woman said. She looked blankly at Allison.

"Would you please call someone to the registration table who knows racquetball?" Allison said coolly.

"There's really no need," the woman answered. "There's nothing anyone can do about it."

"I'll call the tournament director then. I have his private number," Allison said, pulling out her cell phone. "Unless you can get someone over here with some authority." The woman looked at Allison carefully and got up from the desk. She was out of her depth and knew it. They didn't hire her to deal with this kind of crap. She was only supposed to take names and issue credentials.

"I'll go get my supervisor," she said as she left.

"Tony! How are you, man?"

I turned around to see who in the world would know I even existed. I found myself face-to-face with Karl Higgendorfer, the reigning A-division champ.

"Oh… hey, Karl. Good to see you." We shook hands. We hadn't said much to each other in Tempe and I was surprised that he even recognized me here.

"You getting ready for your practice court?"

"Trying. They tell me my practice court is in someplace called Cicero and it was twenty minutes ago," I said, trying to make light of it.

"No way! Is the Ice Queen with you? She'll rip them a new one," Karl laughed.

"Unfortunately she's sick, but Allison's doing a damn good job on my behalf."

Karl looked around me and noticed Allison for the first time. They held each other's eyes for a moment and I could see Allison fighting not to smile at Karl.

"Al-li-son?" he drew her name out emphasizing every syllable. "What have you got yourself into?"

"Hey Karl. I'm substitute Ice Queen today," Allison answered. She was no longer able to hold back the smile and stepped up to Karl. They hugged like old friends.

"Tony, I heard it was this girl who got you in trouble in Tempe. You trust her here?" Karl asked.

"We've gotten to know each other a little better since Tempe," I said. "Lissa picked her to chaperone me in Chicago."

The registration lady was back with an official looking guy in a sports coat and open collared blue shirt. He had a tag on that said STAFF. He pulled us aside and Karl stepped up to the table to register.

"I'm sorry," STAFF said. "I don't know how this could have happened, except that Tony is unseeded and it's pretty automatic to send them to the furthest clubs. We sent Ms. Grant an email on Saturday telling her to take her athlete directly to the club and just give his name for admission."

Allison explained that Lissa had been sick and unable to look at email over the weekend. My phone vibrated as Allison was explaining and, appropriately enough, it was a message from Lissa. It just said, "Sick sick sick. Glad you aren't here!" I showed it to Allison and she turned it so STAFF could see it.

"Please express my sympathy and good wishes to Ms. Grant," he said. "Let me see what I can find later in the day. We may have had a cancellation or a late flight. This will take me a few minutes. We nodded and I turned around to almost plow into Karl.

"I've got an idea," Karl said, "if you guys don't mind. I heard what happened. I've got court time for an hour at eleven. Why don't you join me?" I looked at him blankly.

"Me?" I squeaked. Karl laughed at me and turned to Allison.

"Ms. Perkins, I was pretty disappointed that I didn't get to play against your boy here in Tempe. I've beaten Rob Snyder every time we've met. While I was watching Tony play in the semis I thought sure I was going to get some fresh meat for the finals. Really a tough break with the ankle." He turned to me. "Fully recovered?"

"Yeah, thanks," I said. "I'm taping, but it's pretty solid."

"Then how about a pre-tournament match-up?"

"You've got to be kidding. Why would you want to play me?"

"Well, I've got reasons, and—no offense intended—it's not likely that we'll meet in this tournament. If we both win every match, it would be the fifth round before we meet according to the brackets. If one of us drops to the lower bracket, there's no telling if we'd meet before finals. I'd like to find out what I missed out on in Tempe," Karl explained.

"Karl?" Allison looked at him and dragged him away, just snapping at me to "stay!"

STAFF was coming back with a clipboard and a worried look on his face when Allison and Karl rejoined me.

"I'm sorry," STAFF said. "The best I could get for you was court time here at ten-thirty tonight for half an hour. I know it's not optimal with Tony's first match at eleven tomorrow morning and the banquet tonight, but I'm afraid it's the best I can do."

"It's okay," Allison said, much to STAFF's relief. "We've worked out another solution. Karl Higgendorfer has issued a pre-tournament challenge to Tony Ames during his practice time at eleven this morning. Does the tournament staff have any objections?"

STAFF looked up at Karl and became almost obsequious.

"Mr. Higgendorfer, is this true?"

"Yeah. I understand there's going to be some media guys here and I want to show them how I plan to treat my opponents this week," Karl said. "Tony's my sacrificial lamb."

Shit! What was I into now? Allison agreed to this? There's going to be media watching Karl warm up and he wants to pummel me in front of them? I was about to blow up when Allison grabbed my arm and hauled me away.

"Shut up and don't make a scene. That's my job," she said. "Karl has to talk big. Don't let it get to you. We've got an hour to get you dressed and in focus. Are you with me, Tony?"

She sounded so much like Lissa that my head snapped into the game. I reached for my headset and thumbed in my best playlist. In a second, Queen was shouting "We Are the Champions" into my ears. Allison walked straight into the men's locker room yelling "Cover your dicks!" as she walked through to my assigned locker. Only I heard her mutter, "or don't." She sat me down on a bench and pulled my shoe off to wrap my ankle. She did a good job, too. I had enough freedom of movement to feel like I wasn't playing flatfooted, but enough support to make it comfortable.

As soon as I was taped, Allison slapped me on the rump and said, "Get ready." Then she left the locker room with one last call back to the room at large. "As you were, gentlemen!"

One of the guys caught my attention and I pulled my headset off.

"Sorry to interrupt you, but was that...?"

"The Ice Queen," I completed for him. I nodded and snapped the headset back in place. I saw Karl across the room and a buzz was starting among the players. Of everyone here, the only ones I'd met were Karl and Rob Snyder. I hadn't seen Rob yet. But everyone who Karl spoke to turned to look at me. I didn't know what he was telling people. I was dropping into my zone.

———◁◆▷———

IF I HADN'T had that time on the court with Karl, I'd have died a quick death the next morning. Karl's practice time was in the Plexiglass court so the media could get good pictures of the action. Playing in a glass cube is *nothing* like playing in a regular court. You can't *see* the fucking walls! Karl took me down eleven-to-one in the first game. I didn't feel like I was even giving him a workout. All he did was serve. When we finished that game, Karl motioned both our coaches into the cage.

"Coach, Tony's new at this and you know Allison. She can play the game, but she can't explain it," Karl said. "Could you tell Tony how to see the walls so we can give these guys a good game to write about?"

The older guy grinned.

"You sure you want the competition, Karl?" he asked.

"It's my last collegiate competition, Coach. A guy's gotta have some fun."

Karl and Allison batted the ball around a bit in the fore-court while his coach took me aside. She was feeding him back-hands against the front wall and I noticed how consistent she was before the coach spoke.

"I'm Sim Brown," the coach said. "You can call me Coach. Now what do you see here, Tony." He slapped his hand against the side wall.

"I see glass," I said.

"No you don't," he answered. "You see through glass. You don't see the glass. You could if you really focused on it, but for all your life, you've trained yourself to not notice glass. You see a window, you look through it. You don't look at it. You can't change what you see, Tony."

"That's the advice? I can't see it so live with it?"

"No. You have to *really* not see it."

I had to have looked a thousand questions at him. He chuckled.

"If your coach was here, she'd tell you this. There's no way to explain it without being in the glass cage," Sim said. "Lissa Grant is a fierce competitor. She wouldn't have let you get this far if she thought you depended on the visual reference of walls to know where the ball is going. Think about what you see when you're playing against her. When she serves to you, what do you see?"

"I see where the ball is going to be when I return it."

"Yes! Thank god!" He sounded like I'd just solved the encryption code for the National Defense System and could abort the warheads. Play Tic-Tac-Toe, Joshua. "That's what I mean by not seeing the walls. You have to forget about the walls, Tony. Play the ball where it's going to be." He slapped me on the shoulder, snatched the ball out of the air before Allison could serve to Karl again, and flipped it to me.

"Service!" he called and ushered Allison out of the cage.

I stepped into the service area with a new understanding. It didn't have to do with the walls. It was all about where the ball would be when I wanted to hit it. I served two aces to Karl and when he tossed the ball back to me I saw the grin on his face turn feral. *Now, let's play racquetball.*

With the two-point lead, I traded points with Karl for the rest of the game and took it eleven-to-nine. The third game was what racquetball is all about. We were scoreless after fifteen minutes, and I was up seven-to-six when the coaches pounded on the door to tell us our time on the court was up. It didn't count as a victory, but Karl shook my hand as we stepped off the court and a dozen camera flashes went off. There were easily fifty people watching our challenge match, but most of them were just watching Karl, I was sure.

I'd worked up a good sweat and Allison gave me instructions to shower, hot tub, shower again, and come through to the trainer's room. When I did, she stretched me out on a table and gave my back and front a pounding like I'd never experienced on a massage table before. There wasn't a hard muscle on my body when she was done with the massage.

Well… only one.

Six

A S SOON as i got out of the arena and we headed back to our room, I started texting Lissa and Melody to tell them what had happened during the morning. It was so cool. I knew Melody was still in class, but I expected a response from Lissa. It didn't come for quite a while. Then...

"I'm *so* sick. Boys are running around like crazy. Jack and I are taking turns puking in the bathroom. Wish I was there. Congrats."

I was going crazy. It was just coming up noon on the coast and I waited till it struck before I dialed Melody.

I told her I was worried about Lissa and the boys and what she had texted me. Melody said not to worry and to focus on my tournament. She'd take care of everything.

"Melody, I love you both like crazy, you know that don't you?"

"I know it, darling. But remember, this is your big week. Don't let anything here spoil it. We'll manage; I'll make sure of it. Don't bother Lissa until you hear from me. She doesn't need to be running to the phone if she's heaving in the john."

"I know, Meddy. I miss you."

"Miss you, too, lover. Have fun in the windy city. Hey! Open a window; maybe you'll get a blow job!" I groaned and we finally let each other get off the phone.

When I finally got off the phone, Allison was standing next to the door tapping her foot. We'd changed into street clothes for the dinner tonight and I was expecting to just veg until then. She told me to grab my sports coat and get going.

"Where?" I asked.

"Claude Cahun," she answered.

"Another competitor?"

"In a manner of speaking. Been dead a few years, though. Let's go."

I'M NOT ALL that into photography, but when Allison told the cab driver to take us to the Art Institute of Chicago, I knew I was in heaven. I got so lost in the exhibits—hauling Allison around by the hand and explaining the different styles and techniques—that it was six and we had to rush to the convention center hotel for dinner. What a great way to pull the pegs out from under my nervousness over the match tomorrow.

I met so many people! A lot more of them knew me, simply because they watched Karl's and my challenge match this morning. It seemed that even more had watched the YouTube video that was posted. Guys were coming up to meet me and I'd swear they were sizing me up. There were over 350 competitors, their coaches, the referees, and the staff at the banquet. Yuri Gedov was the speaker. He dominated the international scene three years ago and was one of the movers and shakers trying to get racquetball recognized as an Olympic sport. A little hard to understand, but no worse than Bychkova's Art History class.

A number of people left early and I assumed they were the ones with nine o'clock matches in the morning. Mine wasn't until eleven, so I could sleep in, get a leisurely breakfast, and probably be bouncing on my toes by seven. By the time Gedov's presentation was over, I was bouncing in my seat and Allison grabbed my hand and dragged me out of there.

———— ❦ ————

I CALLED MELODY before bed and she filled me in on the condition of each of our sick loved ones. The boys had been deemed too healthy to stay in the same house as Jack and Lissa. Melody and Kate picked them up after their last class and took them back to Lissa's house.

"Kate's been a life saver," Melody gushed. "I don't think I could have done it alone. The boys are in bed asleep now and Molly will be here before we have to go to class tomorrow morning."

"That's great. But Lissa's still at Jack's?"

"She was in as bad shape this morning as the boys were Saturday night. Don't worry, love. They are both too sick to cheat on us."

"Melody, I wasn't thinking…"

"Of course you were, silly. So was I. I just want her here with me. Instead, she's protecting all of us by staying in quarantine until she's passed the contagious stage," Melody sighed.

"I do wish you were both here with me," I said.

"Instead of Allison?" Melody teased.

"Melody. I'm in competition, remember?"

"Yeah. I just hope I get there while you are still playing. I can't wait."

"Me either."

"Speaking of which…" Melody said. "It's a big lonely house and both Kate and I are used to sleeping with a roommate, so I thought, if it was okay, that we might…"

"You want to sleep with Kate?" I asked. *Shit! So do I.*

"Not actually *with* her. Just in the same bed. Do you mind?"

"Honey, you know how I feel about Kate. You are free to bring her on board."

"Oh, it won't be that." Melody lowered her voice, perhaps afraid that Kate would hear her. "I don't think Kate would sleep with any of us without the others."

"I think I know what you mean, Melody. Treat her well. We'll all be together again soon."

———————◄◆►———————

THE NATIONAL SINGLES competition is a seeded tournament. The first match in each division is between the top player in the country and the last player who made it into the playoffs. When, as in this case, there were seventeen players out of sixty-four who had fewer than thirty points and were there by virtue of having played in a qualifying tournament—like me—there is a drawing to determine the order of the last seventeen places. I was fourteenth. At least I didn't have to face Karl Higgendorfer in his 'warmup' match. Been there. Done that.

I was in the second flight of competitors. Eight courts were used for men's singles, Division A. Four courts had Division B in them. Periodically, women's matches would also be played. Then there was Open Division and Pro Division. It would be five tonight before the second round began.

I got a call from Mom and Dad just as we were entering the arena. They wanted to know what court I was on and let me know they were there and had seats, but didn't know if they were where they should be. I checked the schedule and confirmed that they were in front of the court I was to play on in a couple hours.

When I came out of the locker room, Allison was waiting for me. She took my music player and changed the playlist.

"Lissa says she loaded this playlist for your first match. She wants you to listen to the first song and then you can put it on random or go straight through it or skip things as you wish." I nodded and started listening to the music while I stretched and warmed up.

I wasn't familiar with the piece, but it had a nice Latin rhythm. Just listening to it made me want to sway my hips. I looked at the title but it was in Spanish. I signaled to Allison.

"Do you speak Spanish," I asked, pulling the headset away from my ears.

"Two years in high school. Why?"

"What's this mean?" I pointed to the title of the song: "Besame mucho."

Allison leaned in and listened from one side of my headset and grinned.

"Cesaria Evora. I prefer Andre Bocelli, but I can see why Lissa chose this one. It's much more primal."

"Yeah, but what's it mean?"

"It's a message from your coach," she said. She picked up the melody in a nice voice and sang "Besame. Besame mucho." She looked into my eyes and said, "It means 'Kiss me. Kiss me a lot.'" I grinned. Lissa was here with me. I was going to play some serious racquetball.

The rest of the playlist was all salsa music and I was moving as if I was in a Samba by the time I entered the court. I actually won the toss. That was a first. I started my serve. The walls of my court disappeared around me. All I could see was where the ball was going to be. My opponent never had a chance.

SAM AND BREE had arrived just after my match started and they met up with Allison, my parents, and me after it was over.

"Impressive," Sam said, shaking my hand. "You should thank Karl Higgendorfer for that."

"Why?" I asked.

"The challenge match against him that you won yesterday," Sam replied. "Your opponent went into that match assuming he'd lost already."

"And after this match, you just cemented the opinion," Allison agreed.

"You're kidding!" It never occurred to me that by playing well against Karl in the warmup yesterday would have a psychological effect on my opponents. Well, on me, too.

"When's your next match?" Dad asked.

"Not until nine tomorrow morning," I answered. "If I'd lost, I'd be playing this evening. I can't believe I'm still in." I introduced Mom to everyone. Dad had met them in Tempe, but he didn't realize Allison was filling in for Lissa. He cocked an eyebrow at me and Mom expressed her disappointment that she didn't get to meet my girlfriend.

"Don't worry, Mom," I said. "Melody will be out Thursday night and we'll all have dinner after I finish whatever round I'm playing."

"Well, get dressed, son. Let's all go out to a nice lunch," Dad said. I agreed.

————⊲◆▷————

WHEN I CAME out of the locker room, Bree separated herself from the rest of my entourage and met me at the door. She held out a cloth bag.

"Please deposit your dirty laundry here," she said in a nasal long-distance-operator tone that made me laugh.

"You don't have to do my laundry, Bree. I think I can handle it."

"No way. That's the team manager's job."

"What team and what manager?" I asked.

"The joint college racquetball club that is still looking for a name," Bree said. "And I'm the team manager."

"You can't have a club or a team when there is only one player," I answered.

"Right. That's why I've been recruiting. In addition to you, we now have two men and one woman signed up to start practice in the fall."

"No kidding? Nice job. Anybody I know?"

"Oh, yeah. Remember Tonya?"

"Six-foot-tall women's basketball player?" I asked. "Wicked! But you still don't have to do my laundry, Bree."

"Tony. I owe you and Melody and Lissa a big apology. I was way out of line Friday night. I did some stuff before the party and it turned me into a… it wasn't me," Bree said. So she had been drinking… or something. "The Athletic Director has encouraged me to re-evaluate my life goals and has ordered me to lay off the Welcome Wagon routine. I'm going to do better, Tony. I promise."

"So you really want to wash my uniform?"

"After every match you play this week. I'm really sorry, Tony."

I reached in my duffle and pulled out a soggy shirt, shorts, socks, sweatband, and jock and stuffed them into her cloth laundry bag.

"Okay, manager. We'd better join my trainer, coach, and parents before they leave for lunch without us." Bree linked her arm in mine and we went to join the crew.

I HAD NOT just one, but two great meals, about a hundred text messages from Lissa and Melody, a million laughs with Mom and Dad, and still ended up in my room and ready for bed before ten. I was talking to Melody and Lissa when Allison came out of the bathroom with just her night shirt on. Her bare ass and pussy were prominently in view and instead of getting *into* her bed and hiding them from me, she sat *on* her bed, lifted a foot and started painting her toenails. In that position, her labia parted and I had a view right up the middle.

I faltered in the phone conversation and Melody said, "Tony?"

"Oh… um… yeah. Sorry. I got distracted for a minute."

"Okay. What's she doing?" Lissa asked. The worst of her nausea had passed and she was sounding human again but her nose was still plugged. She'd suggested that she would be home in the morning.

"Well, she's… um… painting her toenails."

"And…?"

"And she's just sitting on her bed. You know, the other one, not mine."

"And…?"

I looked up from Allison's pussy and met her eyes. She had a smirk on her face and shifted positions. If anything, it opened her up even further and I could see the sheen of moisture gathering on her lips. *Okay,* I thought. *I can give as good as I get.* All three of these girls seemed to be asking for it.

"Well, remember what Allison was wearing at the slumber party... I mean when she was wearing anything?" I'll never forget the first glimpse of her in that little short nightie shirt and blue panties, even while I was staring at her naked pussy. "Well, she's not wearing it now. The crop-top she's got on is shorter than her nightie, and I guess the panties were just for show. She says she needs emergency access in the middle of the night or something."

Both my girlfriends were giggling.

"So she's sitting bare-assed in front of you?" Melody asked.

"She remembers the rules of tournament play, doesn't she?" Lissa laughed.

"Oh yeah. She stays on her bed and I stay on mine," I answered. Allison was staring at me with her mouth open almost as wide as her pussy. I don't think she was expecting me to describe her to my girlfriends. "As to her ass being bare, I can only assume so. It's her front that's on display. The thing is I can already see the telltale signs of an impending emergency." With that, Allison put the nail polish on the table and dove under the covers, covering her head as well. "Yep. By the way she just dove under the covers, I'd say the emergency was imminent," I laughed. *Got her, the tease.*

"Well, you need to get some sleep now, Tony," Lissa said. "We've all had enough excitement for tonight."

"But, if you have an emergency of your own to take care of, we could talk you through it," Melody added. "Phone support?" With the visual stimulation I'd had and the lingering scent of Allison's arousal in the air, I knew I wasn't going to sleep without some relief. I turned off the light and snuggled into the bed while I listened to Lissa and Melody for another ten minutes, occasionally answering their questions about my state of arousal. Just at the point of my climax, I heard a gasp and squeak from the bed opposite me.

Hmm. Simultaneous emergencies.

Seven

I CRASHED and burned against the thirteenth seeded player from Loyola Marymount in my first match of the morning. I played well, but I was just plain out of my league. The guy had an incredible match. It made me wonder how I'd ever managed to hold my own against Karl on Monday morning. I guess I just wasn't in the zone. That put the pressure on for my next match. I had no time for remorse, as the next elimination round was at eleven and I was fighting for my life. This was another of the unseeded players who had lost in the first round, but had already fought back through his first elimination match. We were pretty even and I barely pulled out a victory in the last game.

I was able to get a quick bite to eat and a clean uniform, but I wasn't in the mood to socialize with anyone before my five o'clock match. I sat in the stands and put on my headset. I hadn't done any drawing since I got here. Allison and I left right after my match yesterday. Now I had time and the inclination to sketch as I watched the action. I did do a few player sketches, but I found myself daydreaming and snapped out of it when I saw I'd sketched a truly beautiful torso and pair of elegant breasts. I closed my sketchbook and tried to think who those beauties belonged to. When I figured it out, I got hard.

Overall, it didn't help me in what was to be my final match. I met another of the top seeded players who had dropped down at the same time I did. I don't think I'd ever played anyone who was so fast on the court. No matter where I put the ball, he was there. I didn't disgrace myself, but I still lost. My first National Singles was over.

———————◁◆▷———————

I WAS ON the phone with Lissa and Melody when I got out of the locker room to meet up with the rest of the crew. Lissa was feeling tons better and was home with Melody and the boys. Kate was with them, too, and had kept Melody from falling apart while she had responsibility for the boys. Molly had them while the girls were in class and then they took care of all the nighttime rituals and got them to bed before collapsing. After Melody got out of her morning class, she went to pick up Lissa.

With luck, it looked like the rest of us had avoided the contagion. It was nasty, but short-lived.

"Kiss to each of you," I said. "And kiss Kate for me for being such a great help."

"Oooo! Kate!" Melody called. "This is from me because you were such a big help this week." There was a pause and I could imagine the two girls' lips coming together.

"And this is from me," Lissa added. "I would have been lost without help this week." I was smiling as I imagined Lissa placing a loving kiss on Kate's lips.

"Oh, that was nice," Kate's voice came over the phone. "But what about…?"

"And this is from Tony," Melody interrupted. I heard a sudden "oh!" squeak out.

"It takes both of us to give you a Tony," Lissa said. Oh my god! Kate must have been overwhelmed by a two on one lip-lock. I could feel a tightness in my jeans just imagining what that looked like.

"Thank you," I heard Kate tell my girlfriends. "Um… anytime. Really."

"Sounds like you two have your work cut out for you tonight," I laughed.

"Just innocent play," Lissa said. "Unlike what you are likely to have. You're not competing tomorrow, you know."

Damn! I hadn't thought about the fact that I was still sharing a room with Allison and there was no longer a competition prohibition against sex. *Oh man!* I really hoped she was all tease and wasn't expecting too much.

"I might bunk with my folks," I said, softly.

"No way," Melody said. "Have fun, lover boy." I looked up from my conversation and everyone was looking at me, waiting for me to join them. Mom held out her hand for my phone.

"Love you," I said. "I think Mom wants to talk to you." I handed her the phone.

"Hello dears.— No it was very exciting to watch him play.— You'll still come for the weekend, won't you, Melody?— Wonderful— No, of course I won't.— 'Bye now!" Mom disconnected, tucked the phone in her purse and said, "Now we can go have an uninterrupted dinner."

I COULDN'T BELIEVE the dinner. There was a steakhouse near our hotel and the steak was in-fuckin'-credible. I plowed through my appetizer, soup, steak, baked potato, salad, vegetable side, and was ready for dessert. I thought of what Bree had told me on the flight from Tempe and reached over to snatch a bite of mashed potatoes off her plate. She looked up at me and I winked. She actually blushed. I tried the same thing with Allison and she slapped my hand away and told me to order more if I was still hungry. She is really protective about who touches her food!

We had dessert—an incredible hazelnut chocolate torte with Frangelico ice cream for me—and coffee. Bree nudged me and slid her cheesecake toward me to offer a bite, which I accepted and offered her some of my torte. Allison observed what was going on and nudged me from the other side.

"You have got to try a bite of the *crème brûlée*," she said, offering her plate to me. Then to cement the deal, she dipped her fork into my torte and helped herself to a big bite. My mom and dad were leaning in together whispering as they watched the action surreptitiously and almost choked on their laughter when Allison pushed her plate at me.

"Bree," Sam finally said when we were all well-sated, "we have an early flight back tomorrow. We should call it a night. I think we've done all the scouting we can do for this trip. Tony, it was great seeing you on the court. We're going to be proud to have a racquetball club at SCU. When will you be getting back to town?"

"I'm not really sure yet, coach," I answered. I looked at my folks. They were really expecting me to spend some time in Nebraska this summer. I just wanted to be back with Lissa and Melody. "I haven't got my schedule firmed up yet."

"Well, call us when you get back to town. You are the *de facto* president of the club and we need to discuss the formation rules and negotiate court times." Sam shook hands with my mom and dad. "Ready, Bree?" he asked. She gave me a big hug and a peck on the cheek—demure behavior for Bree. She glanced once at Allison with just a hint of jealousy showing in her face.

"Ready, Father," she said and they left the restaurant.

My dad settled up the tab and we headed back for the hotel. Dad was whistling some tune that I sort of recognized and he and mom broke up laughing. Even Allison snorted. When we got to the hotel lobby, Mom and Dad decided to go to the lounge for a nightcap and they hugged us goodnight. He pulled me aside while Mom was hugging Allison.

"You've got a unique relationship with several women," he said quietly. "Don't disconnect from your head. Make good decisions, son." That was the extent of his fatherly advice and Allison and I headed into the elevator while Mom and Dad headed for the lounge.

"Your folks are hilarious," Allison said in the elevator. "Did you hear what he was whistling?"

"I kinda recognized it, but couldn't place it. Some Broadway tune, I think."

"When I'm not near the girl I love, I love the girl I'm near," she sang sweetly. *Really* nice voice, in fact. *"Finian's Rainbow,* 1968, with Fred Astaire and Petula Clark and Tommy Steele as Og the Leprechaun."

"How do you know these things?" I asked.

"Theater major," she said. Then she sang the line again, taking hold of my hand as she did so.

"Yeah, about that, Allison…," I said as I put the keycard in the door.

"Oh shut up and get ready for bed, Tony." She grabbed her night shirt and went into the bathroom. I got second turn tonight, showered the last residue of the day off and pulled my briefs on. When I walked out of the bathroom, I found Allison in my bed.

"Did you get so into swapping food tonight that you want to swap beds now?" I asked.

"Come to bed, Tony. The competition is over. I'm going home tomorrow. Please, come to bed."

I knew this was going to happen. Truth is, I was already half hard when I came out of the bathroom. Melody and Lissa had made it pretty explicit that they expected me to make love to Allison, in fact, *they* would if she'd let them. There was nothing to hold me back. I walked over to the bed and pulled back the covers. When I discovered Allison was naked, I removed my briefs and slid in beside her. She rolled toward me and we kissed with our bodies pressed together under the covers.

Over the past week and a half, Allison and I had explored each other pretty thoroughly with our eyes. There had been a few subtle gropes here and there and the time Melody and I bit her nipples, but for the most part, we hadn't really let our hands wander. Now with all barriers cast aside, we let that kiss linger as our hands investigated each other's body.

Squeezing her breasts beneath my fingers was delightful. Holding her firm ass in my hands was incredible. Feeling her stroke my cock the first time almost sent me over the edge. I nibbled at her nipple and she sighed, pushing my hand down toward the heat of her sex. I was willing to go down on her, but she held me close to her.

"Just make love to me Tony," she whispered. "I'm ready."

My fingers had already told me that she was hot and slippery and she'd smeared my precome over my cock. I rolled over on top of her, feeling her erect nipples raking across my skin as I slid down to get into position.

Allison was beautiful. She was hot. She wanted me. *I want her.* But I kept seeing Lissa and Melody and missing them. I kept hearing my dad say, "Make good decisions." What was it I really felt that was causing me to hesitate, suspended over Allison with my chest grazing her nipples and the tip of my cock touching her moist opening?

"Allison," I said looking deeply into her eyes, "does this feel right to you?"

Eight

ALLISON'S EYES burned into me. I cringed, at least in my head—yeah, if looks could kill. I could almost feel my brain frying. Great timing. Does this feel right?

"I hope you mean: are you hard; am I wet; and is your cock lined up to penetrate my steaming twat?" Allison growled. She thrust her hips toward me, trying to force me into her. I backed off. I wasn't teasing, exactly. *Crap!* What *was* I doing? "I've wanted this for a month, Tony. It feels *good*. Don't get all moralistic on me now."

"I don't mean morally or ethically right, Allison. I'm asking if it's right for us. Are we just going to screw and then go our separate ways? I don't want that."

"Shit! We're really going to have this conversation *now*, aren't we! Damn it!" Allison twisted out from under me and turned away. I saw her shoulders heave. "We're going to talk about feelings and love and the future and when I say 'no, it doesn't feel *right*,' we're not going to do it, are we?"

She shook and sobbed, lying facing away from me, but not far enough for my cock to get the message that it was no longer needed. She felt my hardness and aggressively pushed her butt back into me for more contact. I wrapped her in my arms, spooned behind her.

"Allie," I said, soothingly. "I'm sorry."

She jerked her head toward me, tears glistening in her eyes. "What did you call me?"

"Um… Allie. I'm sorry if you don't like it…"

"In all the time you've known me, you've never shortened my name, given me a nickname, called me by some little endearment. Why now, Tony? Why now?"

"I felt… I'm sorry… I just…" I wasn't being very clear and I was probably sending messages that were as mixed as what I was feeling inside. "Geez, Allison, I don't know."

"Don't stop!" she said, turning fully toward me and pressing herself against me. "Please don't stop calling me Allie. No one has ever…"

"Shhh. It's okay, Allie. I won't stop."

We held each other for long minutes. I was intensely aware of her nipples pressing against my chest and my cock lying against her stomach. We kissed—softly. It reminded me of the sensuous loving kiss she gave me during the contest when she mimicked Lissa. And that got me thinking about my two beautiful girlfriends back home.

"It's the girl thing, isn't it?" Allie whispered to me.

"What is?"

"The thing that's not right. I think the world of Lissa and Melody," Allie said. "And when a girl kisses me, I have to admit that I get squishy inside. Melody and Lissa, especially. But the thought of actually… you know… being with… making love… putting my face down there. Oh god! I just can't imagine doing that. And you three are like one person… well, in a way. No one could possibly be with one of you without being with all of you. And I can't."

Maybe that was it. Melody and Lissa had given me express permission to make love to Allison, fully anticipating a kiss-by-kiss replay when we were together. Somehow, actually being with Allison, though, made me feel apart from Melody and Lissa. It confused the hell out of me. Physically, my erection was straining my limits. Just being cuddled with Allison, I could feel her juices flowing onto my thigh where her pussy was pressed against me. Inside, though, I was aching to share this moment with Lissa and Melody. But that was still only part of it.

"Allie, it's not that, or it's more than that," I began. She delayed my words a moment with another sensuous kiss that we both enjoyed immensely, but then she released my lips and let me continue. "We don't want to lose you. I don't want to lose you," I whispered. "I want you to be my friend and part of my life for a long time, and I'm afraid that once we cross that threshold—both of us wanting more than the other can give—that we'll lose each other. And as to Melody and Lissa," I said looking intently into her eyes, "that would hurt them as much as it would me."

"You are so lucky, Tony."

"I am lucky. I feel like I've won some kind of mega-lottery and I can't even comprehend how rich I am."

We lay there quietly for a while. In our heads, we'd reached the same conclusion, but our bodies were still on a different wavelength. Allison rolled onto her back and I let my hand slide off her shoulder and onto her breast. It was so natural and full in my hand. She moaned slightly and pulled my head back to her for another kiss. Our breathing was coming hard, and I just knew that our bodies were going to betray us, right or wrong. We just couldn't pull ourselves apart.

I felt her hand on my hand over her breast and she tugged it down across her silky muscled abdomen. I felt her thin patch of pubic hair and then the moisture of her slit as she pushed my hand firmly into it.

"Allie…"

"Shut up, Tony. It's an emergency. If we don't do this, I'm going to fuck you whether it's right or not." With that, her hand left my hand to do what came naturally and I felt her fingers wrap around my cock.

Two naked adults, wrapped in each other's arms, kissing passionately, with no reason in the world not to copulate, but still satisfying each other only by means of hand jobs doesn't make rational sense. We'd established a boundary that we could live with and build a future on, though, and when we screamed our mutual orgasms into each other's mouths, both spraying our juices onto the hand and body of the other, we were even closer than we could have been if fucking. We curled into each other, our hands still connecting us, and slept.

Of course, there were two more of Allie's emergencies.

One came early in the morning as my cock slid smoothly between her ass cheeks spooned behind her, my fingers still coaxing her clit to spasm as I came against her back. The other in the shower, covered in soap and shampoo.

Nine

ALLIE LEFT the shower before I did and used the hair-dryer. I kissed the back of her neck as I slipped past her out of the bathroom. I dressed for a day with the 'rents and held a whispered conversation with Lissa and Melody before Melody had to go to class. The two-hour time difference meant that I caught them just after they'd stepped out of the shower.

"Well, lover-boy, how did it go last night?" Melody asked.

"Not like you expected," I said.

"You mean you didn't…?"

"Not exactly."

"This sounds like a good story. Is everything okay, Tony?" Lissa asked.

"Yes, darling. Everything is fine, just not what you were expecting… or at least not what I thought you were expecting."

"I know," Melody said. "Let's wait until I get there tonight and then we can… call Lissa and you can tell us all about it."

"Actually, I'd like that," I said. "I wish you were both here in my arms."

"You cannot imagine how much we wish the same thing," Lissa said. "But if you are okay and Allison is okay, then I guess we can wait for the details."

"I promise, I'll tell you everything," I answered. "I love you."

I'd just disconnected when I looked up and saw Allison standing in the bathroom doorway. She had a towel wrapped around her that barely covered the distance between her nipples and her clit. A sudden move in any direction would make the towel superfluous. What struck me most, though, was that she had dried her hair and it positively glowed as it hung straight below her shoulders.

And the makeup.

Pretty much all the girls I know—or know well enough—look stunning with no makeup at all, in my opinion. That doesn't mean I'm blind, though. When the girls were all made up to go to the gala last Friday in their formal gowns, they were truly amazing. I'm just shallow enough to appreciate the glamour aspect of a little makeup tastefully applied.

Other than at the parties, I hadn't seen Allison wear more than a little eye-liner and lipstick. What I saw now was a strikingly beautiful woman who looked like she could walk down Michigan Avenue and own it. The look was soft but very sophisticated. Before I could say more than "Wow!" though, she was questioning me.

"You really will tell them everything, won't you?" Allison said.

"Yeah. We don't hide anything."

"You'll tell them how I tried to force myself on you?"

"We all have our viewpoints. I'll tell them how I forced myself to stop and how we reached an understanding."

"How you tickled my clit while I stroked your cock?"

"They'll be disappointed. They expected me to tickle your clit *with* my cock. A play-by-play of passionate lovemaking."

"It was." Allison flicked her wrist and the towel fell to the floor. Have I mentioned her tits before? Yeah, I suppose I have.

Still, when an athletic girl as beautiful as Allison stands there naked in front of you, it's hard not to mention them again. And the flat, firm stomach. And the smooth lips of her labia. And…

"Um… Allie? Are you having another emergency?"

"Sort of, but different," she answered. She was serious. "Am I pretty enough, Tony?"

"God, yes! How could you ever doubt that?" I asked. I started to get up to go to her, but she held up her hand to keep me away.

"Would you draw me, Tony?" she asked softly. "Really draw me? Not just a little sketch? Not a group? Just me?"

This was more than a request for a picture. I recognized it. Thank god, I recognized it. Allie understood what happens when I draw. She'd seen the quick sketches I did in Tempe and that was enough to make her want to model the first time. But since then, she'd seen what I could really do. She'd seen the mural with Lissa and Melody. And she'd seen the drawing of Kate. She wasn't asking for a drawing. She was asking me to show her how I see her. She was asking for the connection.

And I was feeling it.

I held out my hand and she took it so I could lead her to the one fully made-up bed. The one we'd slept in last night was a shambles. I pulled the covers back neatly and arranged the pillows. She followed my guidance as she propped herself in the bed and I positioned the pillows from the other bed behind her to provide a little more support. She leaned against the pillows with her left arm over them so that her head was held high. This gave her some support under her upper torso so she wouldn't have to do stomach crunches the entire time she was posing. This drawing was going to take a while.

I covered her with the sheet and blanket, amused at the scowl she gave me. She must have thought I didn't want to look at her body. Then she smiled as I placed her hand on a corner of the sheet and flicked it to her hip where she could hold it comfortably as if inviting me under the covers with her. She naturally repositioned her right leg with the knee slightly bent and drawn up. Her face was already taking on a look of inviting seduction. The final touch was to position her left hand so it was held out to me.

When I stood back, I wanted nothing more than to undress and join her.

"I need some music," I said, reaching for my headset.

"Can I listen, too?" she asked.

"Without a headset, the quality of sound is pretty crappy," I said. I contemplated the problem a minute and then had an idea. "Why don't you sing to me?" I asked.

"Sing what?"

"You choose. Create the soundtrack. Sing me love songs."

"Really, Tony?"

"Mmmhmm." I was already ripping through a warmup sketch with just the key lines that I would base the drawing from—the curve of her hips, the position of her head, the peaks of her breasts, the extension of her hand. She smiled and then began to sing, softly and playfully.

"*Oklahoma*, 1955, with Gloria Grahame as Ado Annie," she said.

> *I'm just a girl who cain't say no,*
> *I'm in a terrible fix*

It was light and whimsical. I sketched rapidly through another warmup, then looked at a fresh, blank sheet of paper.

"Are you sure you want me to sing love songs?" she asked. I looked up to her eyes. There was a pleading look there.

"I want you to sing songs you love," I said. "Sing from your heart." She announced each song before she sang it, as if she was in a recital. I let my eye take in the negative space. Artists all work differently. Sandra starts from a dark background and draws out the highlights. I work from bright white illumination and draw the shadows. Two such different styles. The space between Allie's arm and her body. The space between her breasts. The shadow beneath her chin. The cleft between her legs.

"*The King and I,* 1956, with Rita Moreno and Carlos Riva," she said.

> *We kiss in a shadow,*
> *We hide from the moon,*
> *Our meetings are few,*
> *And over too soon.*

I took time to let my eyes focus on her magnificent breasts. Well, my eyes were being drawn there regardless, so I shaped them in my sketch, used my thumb to caress the curve, blending up out of the shadow, pinching off the definition of her nipple exactly where light met dark. Following the hollow down to her tight abdomen, gently expanding and contracting as she sang.

"*The Music Man,* 1962, with Shirley Jones and Robert Preston"

> *There were bells on the hill*
> *But I never heard them ringing,*
> *No, I never heard them at all*
> *Till there was you.*

I was ready to look at her face. Her makeup highlighted her cheekbones, not in an artificial way, but almost the way

I would use a tortillon to blend the hollow of her cheek into the crested highlight. I looked at her lips as they moved in song and froze them in my mind as I quickly bent to capture what I had seen in that fleeting moment. *Damn, she has a nice voice!*

"*South Pacific,* 1958, with Rossano Brazzi."

> *I'll keep rememberin' kisses*
> *From lips I've never owned*

Her outstretched hand was inviting me to her. She is strong. Forearms ripple with the muscles she flexes when she grips the racquet. But here, stretched out on this bed, the same power is translated to a beckoning gesture, too powerful to be ignored. I reach toward her on paper with graphite in my hand, touching those fingertips and sliding our hands together.

"*The King and I,* 1956, with Rita Moreno and Carlos Riva," she said. Hmmm. I thought we'd done that one, but…

"I thought that was the bald guy… Yul Brenner and… I don't remember the girl. Dad has the album."

"Deborah Kerr. They were the King and Anna. Rita and Carlos played the star-crossed lovers Tuptim and Lun Tha."

"Oh."

"Just listen."

> *I have dreamed that arms are lovely,*
> *I have dreamed what a joy you'll be.*

I moved to the folds and casual draping of the bedclothes, framing her in a background that rippled around her, defining her shape by what surrounds her. That background, the hotel bed, defined where we had not gone. The pillows that supported her were a cushion to her feelings…and mine.

"*Carousel,* 1956, with Shirley Jones and Gordon MacRae."

If I loved you,
Time and again I would try to say
All I'd want you to know.

I'd avoided looking at her mound, where I'd originally drawn three strong lines that defined her shape. Now I let my eyes explore the subtle shapes and contours exposed there. I measured with my pencil on paper the depth of that cleft, the soft bristle of her hair. I walked, in graphite, a path my fingers had found and loved.

"Tony, you're staring at my pussy again." There was a hint of teasing in her voice, but only a hint.

"It's different this time, Allie. I'm drawing."

"What makes it different?"

"I'm memorizing it." She caught her breath and I heard a deep and mournful sigh.

"*Phantom of the Opera,* 2004, with Emmy Rossum and Patrick Wilson."

Say you'll share with me one love, one life-
time…
say the word and I will follow you…

Many artists start with the eyes. They are the window to the soul, as Da Vinci said. Or maybe it was someone else. I guess nobody knows for sure. What I know is that they are where the connection occurs. I'd drawn an entire scene of nine women and had scarcely taken my eyes off Kate's. But for some obscure reason, I'd avoided Allison's eyes as I sat drawing her. Maybe I was afraid of what I'd see there. Afraid of the connection I could feel. But as I sat looking at the unfinished sketch, it was obvious that the time had come. I lifted my eyes and met hers.

I had to memorize a Shakespeare speech in high school as part of my English Literature class. The teacher ruled certain speeches off limits. He wanted no one to ruin his memory of Sir Laurence Olivier saying, "To be or not to be," for example. But he also directed us to other speeches that were less known, but offered a challenge. The Friar's speech about flowers in *Romeo and Juliet*, for example. He'd specifically pointed me to the speech of the Player King in *Hamlet*.

> *But, as we often see, against some storm,*
> *A silence in the heavens, the rack stand still,*
> *The bold winds speechless and the orb below*
> *As hush as death, anon the dreadful thunder*
> *Doth rend the region...*

Seeing Allie's eyes brought me to that moment. I didn't know what to expect, but the suspense of that look took my breath away. There was a deep silence and I simply knew that something awe-inspiring was about to happen.

"*La Boheme*, Puccini."

I had no doubts that Allie had the chops to tackle an opera, but she'd been quoting the movie production and date of every musical she'd sung from so far and I couldn't think of a movie version of *La Boheme* that had ever made it to the big screen.

"*Heavenly Creatures*, 1994, as sung by Kate Winslet," she supplied.

I saw her diaphragm contract and expand three times before the first sound issued from her throat.

> *Sono andati? Fingevo di dormire*
> *perche volli con te sola restare.*
> *Ho tante cose che ti voglio dire,*
> *o una sola, ma grande come il mare,*

come il mare profonda ed infinita...
Sei il mio amore e tutta la mia vita!

I had no idea what it meant, but the beautiful, plaintive tones filled the tiny hotel room and every corner of my heart. I almost forgot to draw as I was sucked into the depths of her eyes—my fingers taking over from my mind and capturing the mist that gathered there, the single tear that streaked from the corner of her eye down her cheek.

It was silent for a moment. We looked at each other, not wanting to move. Then, from outside our door we heard clapping and a man calling "Brava! Brava, Diva!"

The moment was lost and we both snorted.

"Tony, I don't think I can hold this pose any longer."

"Oh, Allie, I'm sorry!" I said. *God!* We'd been like this for over an hour. Her muscles must be killing her. I reached out my hand and lifted her up to a sitting position. As soon as she'd regained her equilibrium she stood facing me, still holding my hand, and still very, very naked.

"Tony, promise me something," she said softly.

"If I can, you know I will," I said. She pulled my hand to her pussy and pressed it there, not asking for anything but the external contact as she held her hand on mine. She pulled my other hand to her breast. It was almost like some formal oath-swearing and not—for all the locations I found my hands—not overtly sexual.

"Promise that when it's right, you'll make passionate love to me, Tony. Promise that on that day or night, whenever it is, that you won't hold anything back."

"I promise you, Allie. When it's right, there will be no reservations," I said. I kissed her lightly on the lips. She pulled back and looked at me with an evil gleam in her eye.

"Swear on the pussy," she said in a low voice that could have come from a 1920s melodrama.

"I so swear," I said, mimicking her tone and giving her mons a little squeeze. She laughed and dropped my hands.

"Look at the time, Tony!" she exclaimed. "If we don't get out of here, your parents will think I kidnapped you!"

Ten

"**I**t's a little late for breakfast," Dad said when he saw us at the door. "Would you like to join us for lunch?"

"Sorry, Dad," I said sheepishly. "I was drawing. The time kind of got away from us."

Dad nodded his head. Mom came to the door, raised one eyebrow at me, and we headed down to lunch. We sat in a little café and it was apparent to me that something was bugging my folks. There wasn't much I could do about it unless they asked something. I certainly wasn't going to provide details about my sex life, or lack thereof.

"When Tony was a little boy…" Dad started. I cringed. This was going to be another embarrass Tony story, I could tell. "He must have been, oh… about ten, I think. He disappeared. He was gone an entire summer day. We called the neighbors, all his friends. No one had seen him. It was beginning to get dark and we were getting very worried." He took Mom's hand and she nodded her head.

"We'd called the sheriff and were on the phone to the police," Mom continued Dad's story. "The minister came to our house and our next door neighbors brought over a casserole."

"That's the Midwest for you," Allie chimed in. "If there's an emergency, there's a casserole." I couldn't see a casserole helping with any emergency of Allie's.

"I looked out the window and Tony was pedaling his bicycle as hard as he could up the road and into our driveway," Dad said. "I never hit Tony in my life, but at that moment I was torn between hugging him and taking my belt to him. The hugging won out, but I had to be stern and lecture him about how worried we were and how worried the neighbors were, and that the sheriff was looking for him. Then the preacher got in on it and he cut me off."

"We're not very religious people, Allison. So the simple fact that the Lutheran minister had stopped by to see if we needed help, was very impressive."

I knew the rest of this story now. I was still going to be embarrassed.

"Rev. Larkin said, 'Tony, everybody is worried about you, but why don't you tell us where you were?' I hadn't even thought to ask that," Dad said. "Well, Tony looked at the preacher and just said, 'I was drawing.'"

I remembered it clearly. I'd been completely caught up in just watching and drawing. It was a point that I thought of now as the first time I'd entered 'the zone.' I just forgot everything around me.

"The preacher wasn't satisfied," Mom picked up the story. "He asked to see what Tony had drawn." I decided to get into the story myself.

"I'd been given a sketchbook for Christmas the year before and some pencils, but I'd never had a particular interest in them. For some reason, that day they just seemed like the most important things in the world to me," I said.

"Tony pulled out the sketchbook and showed us what he'd drawn. The book was full. It was like giving a kid a camera and letting him go, so I'm told," Dad said. "They take pictures of everything, and sometimes they take many pictures of the same thing. The sketchbook was like that. The first half dozen pictures were of the same rock in a stream not far from our house. Then there was a picture of a tree trunk, one of a sign that I recognized as being about a mile from our house, one of the abandoned barn out in Wilson's back forty. There was even a picture of a chipmunk. I couldn't figure out how he'd got the little critter to hold still for so long. It was like Tony was discovering the world in a new way."

"Rev. Larkin quietly leafed through the book," Mom said. "Every once in a while, he'd show us one of the pictures. He just nodded his head, patted Tony and shook our hands. He quoted some Bible verse about the prodigal having come home and to rejoice. Then he left."

"The thing is," Dad said, "we never knew Tony had that talent until that day. Since then, I've never questioned him when he said he was drawing."

And with that, Dad left the question hanging in the air. Mom and Dad wanted to know what I'd been doing all morning (and all night) with Allison. They were completely willing to accept that I was in love with two women, but they were absolutely horrified by the idea that I'd cheat on them. I was getting steamed that my parents were prying into my personal affairs, so to speak. It really wasn't any of their business and I was ready to tell them so when Allison jumped in.

"Did he listen to music while he was drawing back then?" she asked simply.

"No," Dad said smiling. "That came a while later."

"I wanted to listen, too," Allison continued, "but his player doesn't sound good without headphones or speakers, so he had me sing while he was drawing."

"You wouldn't have believed it, Mom," I said. In a few words, Allison had completely defused the situation. What a great girl! "Just when we'd finished, this guy stops outside our door and claps yelling, 'Brava, Diva!' She is really a good singer."

"I'd love to see that drawing!" Dad said enthusiastically. Suddenly, Allison was very shy.

"Um… I'd rather not show you," Allie said. "Tony gave it to me to take home. It's kind of…"

"Oh don't worry, dear," Mom said. "We know Tony paints nudes. We won't pry any further."

"It's unusual, though," Dad mused. "Usually a girl wants a picture of her boyfriend, not of herself." I shrank into my chair. *Dad! Geez!*

"First off, there are two answers to that double-sided question, Saul," Allison said before I could blow up. "The first is that Tony isn't my boyfriend. I'd like him to be, but as much as I love Melody and Lissa, I just couldn't be to them what they'd need me to be. You know, if you date one of them, you date all three."

Oh! Way to go, Allison! I was afraid this was really going to hell, but I chose to stay silent and trust to the goddess beside me that it would come out okay.

"The second answer is that I know what Tony looks like and I have a very good memory," Allison said. "What I didn't know is what Tony sees when he looks at me. No mirror would ever show me that."

Mom was crying. Dad reached over and took my hand. He just nodded his head to me. Mom had to explain, though.

"It wasn't your father, Tony. I really like Melody and Lissa, even though I haven't met them in person yet. And the boys are so precious. I kept your father up all night, and not in a good way. I was so worried about what would happen today when they... when Melody gets here. This week just didn't go the way anyone planned."

"It's okay, Mom," I soothed. I could never stay angry when my mom was distressed. "Allison is our very good friend. Very good. But she would never do anything that would hurt Melody, Lissa, or me. And I wouldn't hurt them, Mom. I'd die if I hurt them."

"Well," said Dad. "I think we should go watch some racquetball, unless you have other plans. Isn't your friend Karl playing this afternoon?"

Racquetball. Ya gotta love it.

I WAS EXCITED. The good thing about having been eliminated from the tournament was that I could take Allison to the airport in Dad's car and pick up Melody when she flew in. Melody's flight was scheduled to arrive at six-twenty that evening and Allison's was taking off at half past eight. We carefully scanned the security lines when we got there to make sure that Allison wouldn't have difficulty making her flight if she waited with me at baggage claim for Melody. It would be a brief reunion, but fun.

With the sexual tension between us relieved, Allie and I were completely at ease walking through the airport hand-in-hand. She had one more year at KSU and wanted to know what tournaments I'd be playing in so she could meet us there. Of course, I had no idea what the schedule would look like. In fact, I almost dreaded finding out. I still didn't know how I was going to handle my class schedule, which was totally screwed up because not only was I pursuing two different degrees in two different colleges, but PCAD was a semester school and SCU was on a quarter calendar. It was going to be a train wreck.

We stopped at a huge board showing arrival and departure times for everything in and out of O'Hare airport to find Melody's baggage claim area. While I was looking down the list of arrivals, Allie shouted from the other end of the board.

"My flight's delayed! It's not leaving until nine-thirty. I don't have to rush away when she gets here."

I laughed as she grabbed my hands and danced in a circle. I was wondering who was more excited about seeing Melody. Okay—stupid question—I was. But Allison was pretty excited, too. Of course, Melody's flight was delayed as well, but only half an hour, so we figured we'd still have a good overlap. We sat with cups of coffee and waited near the exit from the gates for Melody. Man, they can't even make national brand espresso taste good in an airport. Most of my cup went untouched.

"I've got a question," Allie started.

"Should I get one of those guys at the information stand?" I asked before she could continue. She slugged me in the arm. Glad I wasn't planning to play more racquetball this week.

"Those are Moonies, not information," she shot back at me. "I'm serious."

"Go ahead and ask, then."

"I've got a year of school left, but I've been investigating what I'm going to do afterward."

"With your voice, you should be headed for New York. I'd be there for every opening night," I smiled.

"That's like telling a high school girl that with her figure she should go to Hollywood and become an actress. It doesn't work that way. You have to pay more than union dues. Right now, all my credits are college theater. I need professional credits, eventually," she said.

"And New York isn't where you get professional acting experience?"

"No. One of my professors said that trying to make it on Broadway was like trying to get a last minute ticket for the Titanic. Don't get me wrong. It's still the biggest. But theater is happening all over the country now. In fact, there's a dinner theater near where you live that employs nearly one percent of the working Equity actors who are employed on-stage at any given time."

"That has to be the LaRoque Dinner Theater, right?" I asked. I was new to the area, but I was aware of some of the things that went on culturally around town. "Do you think you could get a job there?"

"Maybe. I was wondering… This is a little awkward… I wondered if I'd be welcome if I moved near you. I did a little research while I was there. I couldn't party and play racquetball *all* the time you guys were in class. Anyway, there's not only the opportunity to work in theater, there are also a couple of good graduate programs and a light opera company. But, I'm not sure if I should apply to anything out there because…"

I was up out of my seat and around the little table we were sitting at before she could finish her sentence. I pulled her up out of her chair and wrapped her in a big bear-hug.

"Allie, you will always be welcome near us. Don't ever think we don't want you around. None of us knows what life is going to be like a year from now, but we will always want our friends and family near us." I was hugging her so tightly that she actually pushed me away a little so she could catch her breath. I was about to kiss her when my eye caught something else.

"There she is!" I shouted when I saw Melody coming around security. Then my heart jumped higher than I had. "Both of them! They *both* came!" Allison was right beside me as we rushed to sweep my lovers into my arms.

I shared a deep three-way kiss with my lovers as surprised passengers stepped around us. Allison wrapped her arms around all three of us for a group hug.

"Lissa, you came, too!" I was still so excited that my voice was an octave higher than normal.

"I couldn't miss this weekend with the parents," Lissa said. "Believe me, darling, if I hadn't been so sick I'd have been out here on Monday as soon as the boys started feeling better."

"Besame, besame mucho," I sang, slightly off-key. I'd listened to the song so many times the past three days that I was getting the hang of it. I pulled Lissa to me for a very enthusiastic one-on-one kiss while Melody faced Allison.

Allison's eyes were sparkling, shifting from Melody to Lissa and me and back to Melody. Her chest was heaving as if she was having trouble breathing. Then, as Lissa and I parted and looked at her, Allison pulled Melody to her and planted an enthusiastic kiss on her that so surprised Melody that her eyes popped open in wonder. That didn't stop her from returning Allison's kiss, though. When Allison broke away she was panting even harder and without waiting for anyone's response, she pulled Lissa into an equally hot sampling of her luscious lips. Lissa got a very dreamy look on her face as Allison pulled away.

"Oh god. Oh god. Oh god," Allison panted. "Oh god. That was so good I almost forgot you were girls. God! I wish I could... I want... damn, I love you guys!" And with that she cleansed her palate by attempting to swallow my face.

"Wow!" Melody said. "That was nice, Allison."

"But Allison," Lissa said quietly, putting her arm around the brunette. "We're not trying to convert you. You don't have to do anything with us you don't want to do."

"Tony told me... showed me," Allie said. "I don't know if I can ever *physically* love a woman, but I know that after these two weeks I love all three of you. It's going to be so hard to go home and deal with 150 pre-teens a week at summer camp. All the time I'll be thinking of the three of you."

We collected Lissa's and Melody's bags and then walked with Allison to the security lines for the boarding area. Once there, we had another round of hugs and kisses—a little more demure this time. Just before Allison was out of reach in the line, I reached over and grabbed her hand. She watched as I took her index finger and sucked it into my mouth. Then I held the next finger and Lissa slipped it into her mouth. I could see Allison flushing as Melody took the ring finger into her mouth.

I kissed Allie on the cheek and whispered, "In case of emergencies."

Eleven

WITH THE late flight times, I'd persuaded my folks to wait until breakfast to meet Lissa and Melody. Mom was disappointed, but we would have Friday and Saturday together and then we'd each have to go our separate ways on Sunday. Melody's parents were slated to arrive tomorrow around noon. I just wanted a little time to get reacquainted with my lovers.

There was a man standing in front of our door with a bouquet of flowers. As soon as he saw us approaching he rushed straight up to Lissa.

"Diva!" he exclaimed. "When I heard your singing I could not tear myself away from your door without hearing the last strain. Puccini! So wonderful!"

"I'm sorry," Lissa said. "That wasn't me." Before she could explain, the guy turned to Melody.

"Bella Dona!" he shouted, nearly kneeling before her. "A thousand pardons. I heard only the voice but did not see the beautiful woman who possessed it." I cleared my throat.

"Sir, the singer checked out this afternoon. We are her friends," I said by way of explanation.

"Oh! I am crushed. That voice should be on the stage! I am so sad that I missed her."

"I can give her that message," I said. "We heard you applauding outside the door." The guy blushed a little. He was short—not much if any taller than Melody—with a round physique and balding head. You could see the color in his scalp.

"Thank you," he said. He handed me a card and then offered the flowers to Lissa and Melody. "Ladies, may I leave these in your care. It may not have been your voice, but it was surely your beauty." With that, he hurried away down the hall.

WE INTENDED TO use every second of the night together. Lissa had bought a bottle of bubbly in the hotel gift shop and we ordered a pizza and ate in our room.

Our room. Not in all the time I'd been in Chicago had I considered it Allie's and my room. This was always intended to be *our* room in which Allison was a welcome guest. And, of course, that was the major topic of discussion as we gorged ourselves on pizza. Racquetball be damned; Lissa and Melody wanted a play-by-play commentary on what had happened with Allison. I told them and held absolutely nothing back.

"I can't believe that you had your cock touching her pussy and didn't fuck her!" Melody finally burst out. "I'd have killed you if you did that to me."

"She nearly did," I said, "but it just wasn't right. As soon as she slowed down, she realized it, too. It would have been the last time we'd have seen her."

"You know it was all right with us if you made love to her," Lissa said. "We all wished we could."

"But Allie is really hung up on the girl-girl thing," I said.

"Allie?" Melody said. "That's cute."

"She'd probably join us in bed, but she'd only have sex with me. She just isn't able to cross the physical barrier with a girl," I continued.

"She sure did a good job with that kiss at the airport," Melody said as she sighed dreamily. "I thought maybe she'd made the shift."

"I think she just got caught up in the emotion," I said. "She really loves you both, and she knows how much kissing a girl gets her turned on, but she doesn't want to go any further than that. We have to respect that. You wouldn't push me into having sex with a guy, would you?"

"But we don't want any other guys, Tony," Melody said.

"No. But the thing is, if you did, I'd force myself to do it just because I love you. Afterward, though, I might… no I'd *definitely* resent it. We shouldn't push Allison to do things she's not comfortable with."

"You're right, Tony," Lissa smiled. "We'll be seeing a lot of Allison over the next year, I'll bet. I wouldn't be surprised if we meet at more than one competition."

"She started giving me a list, but I told her she'd have to email it to me," I said. "But it's more than that. She's talking about moving out near us next year."

"She's serious?" Melody asked.

"I think so. She wanted to make sure she'd be welcome to live near us."

"Things could get complicated," Lissa said. "But I do like the way she kisses."

"That's because she kisses like you do," Melody giggled. "It must be like kissing your own reflection."

"Don't be silly," Lissa said. I could tell, though, that she was thinking about it.

"We might need a bigger bed," I ventured. That got me gang-tickled. Not that I minded.

———————◁◆▷———————

THE REMAINS OF the pizza were left on the desk as we took fresh glasses of champagne to the bed. I directed them to the one on the right—my bed. Our clothes didn't make it into the bed with us. When we nested together, you couldn't have told who was on the bottom and who was on top, we were so intertwined—each trying to get every square inch of our bodies in contact with both of our lovers. It felt so good to be next to the two people who meant more to me than anything in the world.

"You know," Melody said—she'd found my cock with her hand and was gently stroking me, "as much as I'm okay with you making love to Allie, there *is* something special about knowing that ours are the only pussies this has ever been in. It makes me all warm inside. And it's the only cock that's ever been in me."

I wasn't sure who I was kissing at the time, Lissa and Melody so completely shared with each other and with me. That's not to say that I can't tell the difference between the two of them, but while we were wound together just floating in our ethereal bliss kissing any one was kissing the other as well. I could tell the difference between Lissa's breast in my left hand and Melody's in my right, but both hands were on my lovers. That was what was important. We were together. The champagne must have been affecting all of us. We'd kiss, stroke, and giggle.

"Are you disappointed that I wasn't a virgin when you met me?" Lissa asked.

"No!" We laughed again. Melody and I had shouted out our answer at the same instant.

"We wouldn't have the boys!" I said. That earned me a kiss from both my lovers. They thought it was sweet, but I was serious. I couldn't wait to get back home to see them.

"And… if you'd been a virgin, we would have had to go out and recruit a different teacher. Who would have taught us all that stuff?" Melody asked.

"Hmm…" I said. "Do you remember when Lissa taught me about cunnilingus, Melody?"

"Oh, darling! The day I forget that, pull the plug. That is the last memory that will be in my mind when I go to the grave. Ohh."

"Speaking of which," Lissa said properly. "It seems that I've been negligent in my duties as instructor, Miss Anderson. Poor Tony has been cooped up in a hotel room with nothing but a stunning brunette with a tightly trimmed pussy and delightfully puffy labia, brimming with feminine essence, for the past three days. He's surely suffered. It is our duty as his loving companions to help him through this difficult time."

I couldn't believe she got that whole speech out. We were cackling at her school-teacher voice so hard we almost missed what came next. Well, actually there was no way for me to miss it. Lissa and Melody squirmed their way down my body and pried my legs apart—not that it took much effort—so they could both lie between them. Melody blew on my already stiffened cock and the cool air caused me to jerk.

"Remind you of anyone?" Melody asked. The rest of my body stiffened, but her little laugh caused me to relax again.

"Now here we have the external genitalia of the male *homo sapiens,*" Lissa lectured. She sounded like a pinch-lipped old English biddy. Everything down there was shaking with my laughter. "Let us start at the bottom, so to speak, and work our way up." She ran her finger along my crack until it came to rest on my asshole. "Anus," Lissa said. There's a difference between shaking with laughter and quaking with excitement, I found. Melody repeated after her.

"Anus. You don't… like… lick it, do you?"

"You can. Our Tony is nice and clean and there are almost as many nerves there as in your tongue. But there are other ways to lubricate the anus outside and it is absolutely necessary to have lubricant for internal stimulation."

"Do you have lubricant handy?" Melody asked breathlessly.

"You have plenty between your legs, darling."

I lifted my head enough to see Lissa's hand dip into Melody's pussy. Melody imitated her and returned the favor enthusiastically. They kissed long and hard. Together they pressed their now well-lubricated fingers against my asshole. I gasped. Nobody had really played there before.

"Just inside, right up here, is the prostate," Lissa said. I moaned as her finger slid into my ass and pressed up against the front of my rectum. My cock jumped. Her finger was immediately replaced by Melody who felt around until she saw my cock jump again. I was already on edge. I wasn't going to last long enough for a blowjob at this rate.

I felt a tongue flick the skin between my ass and my cock.

"Perineum," Lissa whispered. "It's just like ours and you know how you like that licked." A second flick and I heard the echoed "perineum."

"Scro-tum," Lissa said, hefting my ball sack and drawing the word out in her lowest register. It sounded like a troll saying the word. A cute, sexy little troll. "Just a wrinkly old sack, but inside is a treasure." My balls had pulled up tight against me, but the feeling of lips on either side of my sac enticed them down a little. Twin tongues lapped at them until they were hanging loose enough and Lissa whispered, "Testicles."

With that, my two girlfriends inhaled a ball each and brought their mouths close enough to each other that their tongues could touch and dance mercilessly across my nuts. Then Lissa began to nibble her way up the underside of my cock while Melody continued to suck my balls.

"Spongy urethra," Lissa said. How the hell did she make such bizarre, clinical terms sound so sexy? It might have had to do with Melody repeating the word and following Lissa's trail up my penis, nibbling on the part in question.

All lips and tongues suddenly left my cock and I opened my eyes to see my two girlfriends kissing each other while Lissa gently stroked me with her hand. She pulled away from Melody slowly, their tongues seeming to be magnetically attracted to each other even while their lips moved further away.

"Frenulum," Lissa whispered. With that, both brought their tongues back together and ran them up under the head of my cock. *Oh god! It's so sensitive there. And they just tickled it with their tongues.*

I was going crazy. All the attention was being paid to my cock and my hands were just itching to touch my lovers. I petted their hair. It was all I could reach and as they licked at me, they both looked up to my eyes. Their eyes were glazed with lust and I could tell they were as impatient for what came next as I was.

"Glans penis," Lissa whispered. Melody repeated the word as Lissa engulfed the head of my cock in her mouth, bathed it with her tongue and gave just enough suction to make a pop when she pulled off of it, only to be immediately replaced by Melody.

Melody went seriously to work on me then, moving from sensitive spot to even more sensitive spot and back again—sometimes sucking, kissing, licking—making love to my penis. Lissa answered my pleading eyes by crawling up along my body until her lips were next to mine, just brushing me as I tried to capture them.

"The best part about having two girlfriends," Lissa said, "is that you can kiss and have a blowjob at the same time." She lowered her lips to mine and we let our passion use our tongues without words. Well, that might not have been the *best* part about having two girlfriends, but it was pretty damn good!

I sensed heat against my hand and realized Lissa's pussy was pressed against me. I turned my hand toward her and began stroking her moist center, teasing her little bud.

"Is this what you were doing to Allie?" Lissa asked, just loud enough for Melody to be able to hear, too. "Were you teasing her little clit while she stroked your cock? Oh, Melody. He's got his finger in me. Is this how you respond to emergencies? I think it might create *another* emergency."

Melody paused in her ministrations to my cock and I felt her finger join mine inside Lissa. Lissa moaned when she felt each of us inside her. Once she was good and wet, Melody withdrew her finger and a moment later Lissa's moan became a squeal as Melody looked up at me and said softly, "Anus."

"I can't wait!" Lissa gasped and tipped over the edge as we loved her with our hands. As she gasped back to reality, Melody returned to laving my cock with her tongue. Lissa mashed her lips against mine and twined her tongue with my tongue. Then, as she continued to breathe heavily, she moved down my body again. I thought she was headed back to join Mel, but she stopped at my chest. I could still reach and fondle her beautiful breast.

"We're back after that word from our sponsors with the exciting climax of Tony's blowjob," she said, sounding entirely like a television sportscaster. *Oh god!* Laughing did interesting things as my cock vibrated in and out of Melody's mouth and I felt her humming giggle. "Little does Tony know, but the girls have yet another surprise for him." I'd already built up near orgasm a few times and each time they seemed to recognize it and back off just enough to keep me on edge, but I could feel the pressure building and knew it wouldn't be long now one way or another.

And the way had to do with Melody slowly sliding my cock all the way into her mouth and throat and then out again.

"Oh my god!" I screamed. "You can't have just done that! Oh my god!" I could feel the come welling in my balls and everything start to contract. Melody slid back down on me and just as my orgasm hit, buried deep in her throat, Lissa sucked on my nipple and raked across it with her teeth.

I felt my soul leave my body.

Twelve

"**W**HAT ARE we going to do?" Lissa asked. We were cuddled in the bed, hot and sticky from hours of making love, but unwilling to break the contact among us for even as long as it took to go to the shower. The two-hour time change for Lissa and Melody had worked in their favor as midnight didn't seem late and one a.m. was still prime time.

"We could just stay like this and order room service again," Melody suggested. She was completely relaxed and still enjoying having me attend to her right nipple with my tongue as we talked.

"We can do that," Lissa responded, "but you know what I mean. I was crazy without you two while I was in quarantine. Now you're headed to Boston and Tony is going to Nebraska. I have to go back home to my big empty bed. I don't know how to deal with that. You've got me hooked and I want to be with you."

"I felt so incomplete when I was alone," Melody added. "Even with Kate for company, I felt like part of my heart was missing."

"I think that's part of what happened when I was with Allie," I agreed. "It was exciting, but I didn't feel like I was all there."

I'd been thinking about this a lot over the past week. Being in Chicago while Melody was in Lissa's house and Lissa was sick at Jack's had been hard on all of us.

"I don't know how I'm going to face a month in Nebraska without you. Long-distance relationships suck," I continued.

"I suck!" Melody said brightly. We laughed and Lissa and I demonstrated our ability as well as Melody squealed in delight.

———◁◆▷———

WE WERE ALL panting and laughing, catching our breath. There was a cloud of darkness hanging near my mind and I kept it pushed back by immersing myself again in the touch of my lovers.

"Can you meet me in the middle?" I asked.

"I think I just did," Lissa laughed.

"You know what I mean," I insisted. "Come and spend a week in the cornfields of Nebraska?"

"I don't think my parents are going to spring for a plane ticket to visit my boyfriend," Melody sighed. "I can already see the chains being put on my bedroom door when I get back."

"How are your mom and dad doing?" I asked.

"We'll find out tomorrow, I suppose," she said. "It might actually make it easier on me when I'm back in Boston. If they're living separately, they can't watch me all the time."

"I could get a week away," Lissa said. "Jack feels like he really owes us, even though none of the sickness was his fault. My job is flexible and with a phone and laptop the store doesn't really care where I am. But with one of you in Boston and one in Omaha, where would I spend my week?"

"We're going to have to tough it out and get back home as soon as possible," I said. We kissed in pairs and together, reveling in being held and comforted by our lovers.

"Home," Lissa whispered. "Do you really think of it as home, Tony?"

"It's where the heart is, as they say," I answered. "When Mom and Dad talk about us going home for the summer, it seems more like going away for a visit."

"My mom has started packing up our house," Melody said. "I expect it's the last time I'll ever go back to the place I grew up. She wants to put it on the market before the fall buying season."

"Loves," Lissa whispered. "We've talked around this before, but never put the real question in words. I think it's my part to make it explicit." We looked at Lissa and she kissed us both again. "Will you live with me, share my house, and move in with the boys and me? Both of you?"

I glanced at Melody and she had the biggest grin on her face I'd ever seen. I was pretty sure it was reflected on mine. She beat me to Lissa's lips so I settled for nibbling on our lover's neck until she squirmed from the tickling.

"Yes!" both Melody and I told her.

"But we have to share more than your house, Lissa," I said. "It means really being a family. I know Melody and I won't be able to hold down great jobs while we're trying to get degrees, but I have housing and food allowances in my scholarship. I want to contribute to the cost of the household and rent."

"I do, too," Melody said. "We have to pay for housing regardless. I don't want to move in and just mooch off of you."

"Oh, sweethearts," Lissa said. "You know I'd just say don't worry about it, but even from my side, I know how important it is to be partners in this. We'll work it out. I just want you with me."

———————⊰◈⊱———————

EVENTUALLY WE SLEPT, woke, made love again, showered, and met my parents for breakfast—on time.

Mom was great! She walked right past me and swept Lissa and Melody together into a hug that had 'family' written all over it. She didn't hesitate trying to figure out protocol over whether to give the oldest, prettiest, closest, or friendliest girl first greeting. She captured them both and pretty much dragged them away from me toward their booth. Dad grinned and gave me a hug before turning to look at the women.

"We'll be lucky to see any of the three of them for the rest of the day," he said.

"But Dad, you haven't met Melody yet." I dragged Melody out of Mom's grip for a minute and said, "Sweetheart, I have two parents and you have to meet Dad, too. Dad, this is Melody; Melody, Saul."

"I'm so happy to meet you both in person!" Melody squealed, hugging my father.

"Hi, Saul," Lissa said, coming back to him. "It's good to see you again." Dad gave as good as he got when Lissa and Melody hugged him and we finally got settled.

"Well, I guess I don't have to introduce anybody to Mom," I said. She'd positioned the girls on either side of her, leaving Dad and me to share the bench on the other side of the booth.

"Oh, we're old friends now," Mom said. "I talk to these girls more often than I do my own son." My eyebrows shot up. I had no idea they were talking to Mom that often. "Now, how are the boys?" she asked.

After the Intercollegiate and our experience with Melody's parents, we decided that we had to tell my folks about the boys right away. We'd sent them the same picture that we sent to Mr. Anderson and they were just as excited about having two little boys to dote over as at my having two beautiful girlfriends.

"I hope you don't mind us coming for a little visit this fall," Mom said. "I so want to meet everyone!"

"Why don't you come for Thanksgiving?" Lissa asked. "That will give time for Tony and Melody to get settled back in school, and I'll be done with The Open. It's in October and things will be pretty crazy before that."

Just that quickly it was agreed that my folks would visit us for Thanksgiving. I thought that was pretty cool. My parents were coming to visit my girlfriends and me in *our home* for a holiday! *Wow!*

Mom and Dad were pretty amazing. I'd never doubted how much they loved me and supported me, but my first year in college had left me in such a deep depression that there were times I couldn't force myself to pick up the phone to call them. I got so caught up in feeling like I had to be independent and that calling home was a sign of my failure. With Melody and Lissa's help, I realized that part of my depression was feeling cut off from the incredible support I'd always had from my family. I loved them like crazy and I was sure my being away at school had been as hard on them as on me.

After we'd caught up with how the boys were doing now that the illness had passed, we ordered breakfast and caught up on everything else, including my parents having to deliver a blow-by-blow description of my four matches.

"I really want to go back over for the finals tonight," I said. I hadn't felt compelled to sit through every match up to this time, but the Division B finals would be at 3:00 and 4:30, the women's Division A final at six-thirty, and the men's at eight o'clock. I definitely wanted to be there for the last two.

"How many tickets will we need, then," Dad asked. "I'll call over and reserve them."

"Allison left Lissa her credentials, and Coach Jacobson left his for you, Dad. So we'll need tickets for Mom, Melody, and the Andersons."

"Oh, yes. And when will your parents be in, dear?" Mom asked Melody.

"About noon," Melody said and then hesitated before going on. "I don't know if they'll go to the game tonight or not. My parents are... um... not as... accepting as you are, I'm afraid."

"Don't worry, we'll work on them," Mom said firmly.

"Well, Mom has really come around, but my father is a different matter. Mom doesn't really stand up to him and I just don't trust what will happen when they're together. With the divorce and everything, I don't know..." Melody shrank down in her seat and looked longingly across the table at me. I reached for her hand, but Mom was there before me and pulled Melody to her like a daughter.

"Don't you worry, dear," she said. "It will be all right." She held the embrace for a moment and Melody sighed. Then Mom excused herself and Lissa moved to let her out.

"I see I made a foolish mistake when I forced you both to sit with me. Tony, go sit with your girlfriends so I can have my husband," Mom said, shooing me out of my seat. I don't know if she expected me to get between them, but she just smiled when Lissa slid to the middle and hugged Melody, then turned to me and did the same.

"It really is," Mom said quietly as she gripped Dad's hand. I looked at her curiously. Dad took over the conversation.

"That wasn't a set-up," he started. "But Deborah and I don't have a lot of experience with... shall we say... arrangements like yours. So we've done quite a lot of reading in the past few weeks. Do you know that literature is full of threesomes, but most are of the sort where two women share a man or two men share a woman? They are almost without exception two-on-one arrangements. We weren't sure what to expect. We thought you would automatically both move to opposite sides of Tony. But you are truly all three in love with each other. It's beautiful."

We looked at each other and none of us could imagine any other way it could possibly be. At the same time, there was a palpable new level of acceptance on my parents' part. We decided that it was time to tell them about our plans for the fall.

"It's going to be a hard summer on all of you," Mom said when we'd told them of our plans to move in with Lissa. "We want Tony to be with us this summer, too, but we promise not to keep him away too long. Now that I actually see the three of you together, I can't imagine what it must be like for you to be apart."

As MUCH AS i wanted to spend all my time in the presence of my girlfriends, and as much as I wanted to share them with my parents, I had another task in mind and I suggested that we spend the couple of hours until Melody's parents arrived doing a little shopping on the Loop. I held a quick whispered conversation with my mom on the walk over to State Street.

"Oh, look!" Mom shouted as we approached Washington and State Street. "Macy's is having a sale! Surely you boys can give us a little bit of girl-time, can't you?" Dad and I laughed and sent them on their way, promising to meet back at the corner in two hours.

"So, shall we just stand here and see how many people we know?" Dad asked. He'd told me a long time ago that if you just stood at State and Washington in Chicago for an hour at any time of day or night, you would meet someone you knew. I didn't have any idea if it was true, but I had a different mission in mind.

"I need your help picking out a couple of little gifts," I said. "That's why Mom shanghaied the girls."

"I had a feeling there was a plot under way," he laughed. "Lead on!"

I'd had some time before Allison left to do a little Internet shopping and found a store just off Michigan on Washington that had what I thought I wanted. When we entered, it was like going into another world. The Loop, especially when you are right under the El on Washington, is noisy. The trains are loud and everyone on the street is shouting to be heard above them. Add the traffic noise and homeless people trying to get your attention and you really can't hear yourself think. But when we walked into this jewelry store, all the noise was left outside.

Thick carpet muffled our footsteps as we approached the counter and a very pleasant middle-aged woman approached after we'd had a chance to survey our surroundings. She was friendly and spoke in an equally muffled tone so as not to disturb anyone else around.

"Good morning. I'm Miss Hayes. May I help you gentlemen find something in particular, or would you prefer to browse?" she asked pleasantly. Under other circumstances, I'd have bolted right then and there. Everything about this store screamed more money than I'd ever see in my lifetime, but I did have a savings account and was sure I had funds enough to cover the purchase. The problem was that I didn't have cash or a credit card.

"May we have just a minute to consult and then ask for your assistance?" I asked. She acquiesced and moved a respectful distance away while I turned to Dad. He raised an eyebrow at me, waiting.

"Dad, I need to make a purchase, but a place like this isn't going to take my check and I don't have cash. Can I borrow your credit card and pay you when we get back home?

"Ahh. So that is why you wanted me along. Front the bill. How much are we talking about?"

"About a thousand dollars." Both his eyebrows shot up.

"Are you really ready for this, Tony?" he asked. I swallowed hard and nodded my head. He looked me straight in the eye for a few seconds and I knew not to waver. Then he nodded and said, "Okay." I approached the saleslady.

"Excuse me," I said. I pulled out my phone and called up the picture I had downloaded from the Internet. "I'm interested in this." She looked at the picture and then back at me in surprise.

"You are aware that piece of jewelry is often for groups… of… uh… three?" I nodded my head. She made a slight gesture to my dad and me and looked the question at me.

"No," I said. "This is my dad. He's helping me with the purchase."

She moved back behind a display case and opened a drawer beneath a display of necklaces.

"What configuration would you like?" she asked. I'd only seen one picture, so I wasn't sure what she meant. She went on, "We have it with two gold and one diamond, with two diamond and one gold, and with three of either."

"Oh! I'd like the ones with two diamond settings and one gold. And I'll need…"

"Two of them," she finished for me. "We don't sell many of these, but we never sell just one." She produced two velvet boxes and opened them. The contents were identical. Two diamond studded hearts were interlocked with one in gold. I snorted a little when I saw them up close. It was the first time I realized that they looked a little like a daisy chain. "Not right?" she asked, noting my reaction.

"Oh no!" I hastened to correct her. "They're perfect. I'll need two 16-inch simple gold chains, as well."

"Not going to let them hide it," she laughed. "I think we can fix up exactly what you need. Monique?" she summoned another saleslady. Monique was both younger and more slightly built than Miss Hayes. The older woman quickly threaded one of the pendants on a chain and lifted it to fasten around Monique's neck. I could see right away that it wasn't quite right.

"May I suggest," Miss Hayes said as she demonstrated by holding the ends of the chain at different positions on Monique's neck, "that you either go with an eighteen-inch chain so the pendant clears the collar bone, or try a fifteen-inch chain so that it nestles in the hollow of her throat. If you find that it's not quite right after you've presented it, I'll be happy to trade it for the correct size or cut it if necessary."

We agreed on the shorter chain. I thanked Monique for modeling it for me. Miss Hayes wrote up the sale and changed the necklaces from a pendant box to a long narrow box for bracelets and necklaces. The presentation looked divine. I declined gift-wrapping.

"This is a lovely gift for two special women," Miss Hayes chatted as she ran Dad's credit card.

"Oh believe me," Dad said, "the young ladies are every bit as lovely as the jewelry." She raised her eyes to me.

"You are a very lucky young man on several counts," she smiled. "I wish you... shall we say... triple happiness."

I slid the bag into Dad's jacket pocket before we went to meet the girls and told him I'd get them later. I described what I wanted to do and Dad got that kind of crooked smile on his face that parents get when they can't believe what their kids want, but do it anyway.

Thirteen

"**M**ELLY!" LEXI said as she approached us across the hotel lobby. When she released her mother from a hug, Melody went on to the formal-looking man behind Lexi and greeted her father. *Who wears a suit on vacation?* I thought.

"Hi, Daddy," she said, smiling at him. He didn't hug her, but put both hands on her shoulders and leaned forward to kiss her forehead. Lexi had moved on to give Lissa a hug and then smiled at me and did the same. She glanced over her shoulder as if to make sure her husband had seen. Melody took her father by the hand and led him to Lissa.

"Daddy, this is my girlfriend, Lissa." He held out his hand and Lissa shook it but he didn't say a word. "And this is my boyfriend, Tony." He repeated the gesture. His handshake was as neutral as any I'd ever had. There was nothing aggressive about it, but certainly nothing friendly, either.

"Mr. Anderson, Lexi," I said, "this is my mother and father, Deborah and Saul Ames."

My dad stepped forward to shake first Mr. Anderson's hand and then Lexi's. Everything was silent and I had visions of catastrophe playing behind my eyes. Then Mom stepped into the breach.

"Oh, the girls have told me so much about you both!" she said, ignoring Mr. Anderson in all but her comment and immediately hugging Lexi. "I feel like I'm meeting old friends. What an exciting time. Have you checked in? We've slated a late dinner so we can all go to the final match of the tournament tonight."

"I thought he was eliminated," Mr. Anderson said. I thought he sounded just a little too hopeful about that.

"I'm out of the tournament," I said, "but a friend is playing in the final game for a repeat Championship. We're planning to see that."

"It was so cool, Dad," Melody jumped in, trying to engage her father in something to break his apparent bad mood. "Tony played Karl in a challenge match before the tournament started and it's all over YouTube. It was amazing. Tony was ahead when they had to stop playing."

"But you didn't make it to the finals?"

"No, sir. I had a great game against Karl before the tournament, but I just didn't have the experience and stamina to hold it together against the competition for the long haul."

"That should be a lesson to you," he said, scowling at me.

"Daddy, stop it. Be nice."

"Melody, I'm here because you wanted me to meet these people. Fine, I've met them. They seem very nice. But you have to face reality, sweetheart. This relationship is doomed from the beginning."

"Doomed from the beginning?" *Oh shit!* The last time I heard my mom use that tone of voice it was immediately followed by "Tony, you're grounded." But she'd swung her focus fully on Melody's father. The guy didn't know what he was in for.

"Doomed from the beginning?" she repeated, advancing on the man. He stepped back a pace, but Mom kept coming.

"And exactly how is that worse than when you discovered *your* relationship was doomed?"

———————◁◆▷———————

WAY TO GO, Mom!

Have I mentioned how much I love my mom? She's almost a foot shorter than Mr. Anderson, but I swear he went from six-foot to four-foot in 0.2 seconds. Mom was towering over him and going for the *coup de grâce* when Dad stepped up beside her and kissed her cheek. He turned her smoothly away from Melody's dad, but she was replaced immediately by Lexi.

"Oh, Harold. Don't be such an ass. We came here to meet Melody's friends and family. Do be civil." I don't think that Lexi had ever contradicted her husband based on what Melody had told us. He was still trying to form words when Lexi turned to Lissa. "How are the boys, Lissa? Is Jack coming out this weekend?"

Wow! By the expression on his face, it might have been dawning on Mr. Anderson that he'd lost, but I wasn't sure if he realized how much he'd lost.

"Oh the boys are doing fine now," Lissa answered. "Kids recover from these things so much faster than adults do. Kate and Molly agreed to take turns with them this weekend so I could come out here with Melody and Jack could continue to recover. I think he got hit hardest of the four of us and he's just getting back to normal. You have his phone number, don't you? You should call. I know he'd love to hear from you."

"Why don't we let these kids go save us seats at the arena," Dad suggested. "The four of us could have a mid-afternoon cocktail before we join them." Dad is one of the best peacemakers I've ever seen. I've never heard him raise his voice, even in his classroom. He had Mr. and Mrs. Anderson in tow with him and mom and waved the three of us off to the games.

I looked at Melody and Lissa and all three of us heaved a sigh of relief.

"Well, that went better than I expected," Melody said, rolling her eyes to clue us in on her sarcasm. "What a shit!"

"Mel, honey," Lissa soothed, "we knew from the phone conversation a few weeks ago that he was going to be a tough sell."

"At least he didn't take me hostage and drag me off the airport," Melody sighed. "Tony, your mom and dad are *so* nice. Wanna trade?"

"I don't think we actually get to trade in this situation," I said. "I think we have to share. Both."

"For better, for worse," Lissa said. Melody and I looked at her expectantly. When Lissa realized what she'd said she blushed and we all started laughing.

"Darling, that almost sounded like a proposal," I said as we headed off to the arena.

———⊲◆⊳———

THE MATCHES WERE great. By the time our folks joined us, it was almost time for the men's final. Dad was in rare good spirits and I wondered how many afternoon cocktails they'd all had. Mr. Anderson seemed a little mellower. He'd lost his tie, at least. Mom and Lexi were gossiping together like they'd known each other a hundred years. They all enjoyed the match, but I was spellbound. Karl was phenomenal, of course. But this guy, Brian Summers from Clarkson University out East, was a demon.

"That's who you'll have to beat to win the championship next year," Lissa said to me. She leaned in close and made sure I was seeing his "isms" as well as the unbelievable plays he was making. Karl fought through to eke out the championship by two points in the last game.

"How did I ever get ahead of Karl when *I* played him?" I asked, shaking my head.

"You haven't watched the video yet, have you?" Lissa asked. I just shrugged and shook my head no. "It's going to be part of your training this fall. Probably for your whole club. Your little challenge match got 25,000 hits on YouTube before we came out here. It's probably double that by now. But this one will have three times that number. It was no more amazing, but it will have the title attached to it."

"This will be on YouTube?"

"I'm sure someone will figure out a way to put it up there, but it will be on ESPN and USAR websites by morning. Yours will be pulled up a lot as we head into the fall."

"Why would anyone want to watch me play when they could see this?" I asked. This was a match that I'd be spending hours watching. It was like going to racquetball school and seeing the masters teach a class.

"Brian is a junior. That means he'll enter next season as the number one seed and national silver medalist. Karl is the unifying gauge of talent," Lissa explained. "Any time a competitor draws a match with someone Karl played in this tournament, they'll view that video. And then everyone will view the video of Brian playing him to see how it's different. They'll all figure they have to beat Brian to get to the podium. But once people start seeing your match with Karl, they'll start comparing the two. They'll be able to see exactly how you both played against the same champion and no one else will count. The target on your back is almost as big as the one on Brian's."

"But I'm only…"

"…only a freshman," Lissa supplied. "That's what makes you so dangerous. You've got at least three years of eligibility ahead of you. You are the biggest threat to any upper classman ever getting to that podium."

"Shit."

———◄◆►———

WE HAD CHICAGO Deep Dish Pizza at for dinner at Pizzeria Uno. These guys *really* know how to make pizza. We had to wait forty minutes to get in and the pizza didn't arrive until nearly an hour later. By that time, we were all so hungry that we'd gone through the breadsticks and the older folks had finished two bottles of wine. Lissa had a glass, but switched to sparkling water before things started getting rowdy.

We walked back to the hotel in a ragged line and it seemed like there were a lot more jokes being told than were being laughed at. When we got into the hotel lobby, things took a turn for the worse. I was wondering when the other shoe would drop, so to speak. It was a big shoe when it fell.

"Melody, you and your mother can go to our room while I have the bellman get our bags and deliver them," Mr. Anderson said as we were all hugging Mom and Dad goodnight.

"That's okay, Dad. I have a room of my own with Tony and Lissa," Melody answered sweetly.

"Not in my house!" he bellowed back at her.

"This isn't your house," Melody shot back. "And I won't be staying in any house that doesn't welcome my lovers."

"You will get yourself in line right now, young lady. This has gone on entirely long enough. I'm not having any daughter of mine shacked up with two… two… people," he finished weakly. But Melody was all over it now and I wasn't going to get between her and the object of her wrath.

"Why don't you just go back to Boston and forget about me, then," Melody shouted. "It's obvious that you don't care enough to even give us a chance. I'll go back with Lissa and Tony."

"You most certainly will not. Alexandra…" he turned to address his wife.

"Oh stow it, Harold. Melody has a good idea. Go back to Boston and let the rest of us enjoy our weekend," she said.

"Alexandra! How dare you challenge my authority?"

"That's been the problem for the past twenty-five years, hasn't it Harold? I never challenged your authority. Well, listen here. You walked out on me, on our marriage, and on our family. It was your choice. *My* choice is not to lose my daughter. And for your information, I'll have my *own* bag delivered to my *own* room. There's no reason I can think of that I would spend the night with my *ex*-husband!" Melody's mouth hung open. I don't think she'd ever heard her mom stand up to her father like that. And the way Lexi said "ex-husband," you could see that he'd driven the final nail into his own coffin. Lexi was flushed and panting.

Mr. Anderson looked at all of us. Lissa and I had our arms around Melody and Lexi had moved over to stand beside us. My parents, wisely, were staying in the background to let the scene play itself out. He turned on his heel and disappeared into the lounge.

We looked at Lexi and tears were running down her cheeks. Melody wrapped her arms around her mother.

"Oh, mom! I'm so sorry. I didn't mean to ruin everything for you."

"Hush now, Melody," Lexi said quietly. "I'm sorry I never stood up to him before. I was a terrible mother. It's me that needs your forgiveness. I love you, Melly."

My mom and dad came up and Dad laid a hand on Lexi's shoulder.

"Would you like me to go talk with him?" Dad asked. "Maybe I can talk some sense into him."

"No. Thank you, but no," Lexi said. "It's run its course. I only just realized that it's truly over."

"Anything we can do," Mom said, "just let us know."

"There is one small thing," Lexi said softly. "I don't actually have a room of my own here. Do you have a spare bed in yours that you'd loan me?"

Mom laughed.

"Of course. Let's go get your bag and let the children get on with their lives. Saul, why don't you get us a bottle of something?"

"Hmm," Dad said, considering. "Two women and a bottle of something in my room tonight? Like son, like father, I guess." That earned him a swat on the shoulder and he laughed as he left to hit the nearest liquor store.

We got Lexi's bag from the bell station and she went with Mom. Melody, Lissa, and I went up the elevator to our little room breathing a sigh of relief and leaning heavily into each other.

Fourteen

A **BOTTLE** of champagne was on ice in our room with three glasses and a box of dark chocolate truffles. The truffles were my Dad's idea and he'd taken care of it.

"More of Allie's admirers?" Lissa asked, surprised. I acted all innocent and just shrugged my shoulders.

"Was she singing or having an orgasm?" Melody asked. "Mmm. Truffles!"

We decided to take a shower before we indulged in any kind of decadence, but the lure of champagne and chocolate—and our overfilled stomachs from pizza—kept our libidos in check while we all showered together. Not to say we didn't do a lot of fondling and kissing and the girls felt it was absolutely necessary to be freshly shaved tonight, so I shaved and then realized they meant themselves, so I shaved again... and again... and made especially certain that everything was perfectly smooth.

We came out of the bathroom fresh, steamy, and slick. I opened the champagne like my dad taught me. "Son, the cork should come out of the bottle like the sigh of a contented woman." So, there was no explosion or cork flying across the room and precious drops of wine spilled on the floor.

"Okay, before you get your champagne, you have to stand between the beds and face away from each other," I directed.

"What's this for, Tony?" Lissa asked.

"You knew about all this being here, Mr. Devious," Melody chimed in.

"I have a surprise for you. Now here are the rules. You can't move away from where you are. After our first toast, you can't turn around and look at anything else. You can't use your hands for anything but your champagne glass. And you can't say anything—although I'll make an exception for general moans and sighs," I instructed.

"You're sounding kinky," Melody said.

"Fun!" Lissa volunteered. I handed them each a glass of champagne and we touched them together.

"Here's to my true loves," I said.

We all took a sip. I positioned them back-to-back with just enough room between for me to squeeze in. I set my glass on the bedside table. I reached around Lissa and hugged her to me, letting my hand trail lightly over her torso.

"The limitation of having just one boyfriend, my loves, is deciding who gets to come first," I said. My fingers dipped down into Lissa's pussy and she groaned, leaning back into me. I could hear Melody sigh. "You, my love," I continued whispering into Lissa's ear and tickling it with the tip of my tongue, "came first last night. So it's Melody's turn tonight." I tweaked her nipples slightly and Lissa squeaked but kept from saying anything. Then I turned and embraced Melody.

"My dearest Melody," I began. "You were the first to teach me about love. You helped bring me back to life and show me a light—a way to be happy." I stroked her sides and cheeks, quickly down her legs and back up the inside, gliding past her sex and looping lightly around her breasts before I let my fingers slide up the curve and lightly pull at the nipples. While Melody was moaning, I pulled the first necklace out of the drawer of the bedside table. I held it so she couldn't see what I was doing, just in case her eyes were open—which I doubted.

When I pulled the chain around her neck and she felt the weight of the pendant on her throat she let out a little involuntary "Oh!" but she stopped short of saying anything else as she reached up to touch the jewelry. I caught her hand and prevented her from touching it. "I will always love you," I said as I pulled her hand down and allowed my own to return to her center, probing gently and sprinkling kisses down her neck and across her shoulders. This elicited a long drawn-out moan followed by a plaintive yip when I withdrew.

I turned to face Lissa's back again and let my fingers caress her ears and down her neck and shoulders.

"Already?" she asked.

"Shhh," I said as I continued exploring her body. "Lissa, you made love blossom, taught me how to love a lover or two, helped me find the skills to fight being out of control all the time, and made me a part of your family. I've never been so happy in my life." I reached for the second necklace and drew it up beneath her chin and fastened it. She hadn't stopped making little squeaking noises since I caressed her breast and they increased in volume as my hand neared her core.

"Lissa," I said as I stroked lightly across her pussy, "I will love you forever." She pushed her head back to rub her cheek against mine and I kissed it. I stepped back just far enough to reach around Melody and begin turning the girls to face each other.

"My darlings," I said, "you are my happiness and I love you."

By this time, they were turned far enough to face each other and their eyes went immediately to the other's throat where the triple heart nestled. It was like watching one of those games of mirror that people play when one tries to mimic exactly what the other is doing. Their right hands reached out to touch the pendant at the other's throat while their left hands reached up to touch their own, putting two hands on each pendant, with a champagne glass caught between. They leaned forward and kissed each other softly. Their eyes sparkled as both girls turned toward me.

"It's beautiful!" they both exclaimed and my face was instantly covered in kisses and my lips sought out two pairs of lips that tasted of heaven. We all walked over to the big mirror on the closet door so we could look at them together. Then champagne, necklaces, and chocolate were all forgotten as I was pushed back onto the bed and buried under a squirming mass of naked girl. It seems the daisy chained hearts were an inspiration to all of us.

It was a very good night.

———◁◆▷———

I'D LIKE TO say the morning was just as great, but when we all gathered together for breakfast, we discovered that Harold Anderson had checked out of the hotel and left. That sobered everyone's mood, though Mom and Lexi oohed and ahhed over the girls' jewelry. You'd think I'd just given them both big diamond rings as excited as everyone was. My dad looked at me and I really felt like he was proud of me. It was such a cool feeling!

The girls also decided that it was unfair that I didn't have a piece of jewelry and decided that we needed to go back to the shop. I said that I really couldn't wear that particular piece because it was too feminine. I had enough trouble with people thinking I was gay. Lissa reminded me that no one who saw me with the two of them would think I was gay, but I still thought the pendant was a little too much.

Miss Hayes was at the jewelry store and immediately came to me to ask if I needed to exchange the chains. She stopped as she looked at the two women with me and just clucked her tongue a bit. "Lovely," she said. "Just lovely." I wasn't sure if she was referring to the pendants or my girlfriends. But once she heard what they wanted and my objection to the triple heart pendant they wore, she nodded her head and went to her office. She returned a moment later with a large photo album of custom jewelry from a variety of different craftsmen. Of course, Lissa wanted to stop on every page, but Miss Hayes had something particular in mind.

The picture she showed them was of a heavy linked chain that had an intricate pattern in the way the links were assembled. But at the center of the chain was what she referred to as a Celtic heart. Instead of three hearts, it was a single heart wrapped in a trefoil of leaves. It was all hammered silver and I agreed that it was manly. Melody and Lissa asked me if I would wear that on my wrist. *God, yes!*

Of course, it was a special order item from some custom jewelry-maker in Oregon and they decided to have it shipped to Lissa's house.

We spent the afternoon at the Art Institute of Chicago where I pulled my entire extended family from exhibit to exhibit, having already been there earlier in the week with Allison.

———◁◆▷———

SUNDAY MORNING WAS difficult. We drove Lissa, Melody, and Lexi to the airport and I tearfully kissed my girlfriends goodbye.

We agreed we'd be back at Lissa's house in just a couple of months, but the agony of waiting that long seemed unbearable.

I asked Dad if I could drive first when we headed west and he agreed. Paying attention to the road was the only way I could keep my mind from sinking into self-pity. I didn't want my parents to see me cry as I thought about Lissa flying west and Melody flying east.

It was ten long hours to Nebraska.

Fifteen

"**T**ony!" **Damon** yelled into my ear. I held the phone away slightly. I'd surprised the boys by calling to read them a bedtime story over the phone. "Did you go away?" he asked.

"Just for a while, buddy," I explained. "I needed to come and visit my mommy and daddy."

"Meddy is with Gramma Lexi," Drew supplied. He was already sounding more grown up than when I left him.

"When you coming home, Tony?" Damon asked. "We miss you." I almost broke down crying.

"Soon, buddy. Soon."

I'D BEEN HOME for almost two weeks and the dark clouds of depression were weighing on me. Everything in my room seemed slightly foreign and juvenile to me, from the little twin bed to the art posters, to my desk and model airplanes I'd made as a child. The only thing that seemed right was my easel on which stood my latest painting.

I'd worked slowly on the oil painting. It wasn't dry yet, but I kept a cloth over it, held away so it didn't touch the wet paint. I wasn't ready for my parents to accidentally walk in and see it. Still, I could see clearly in my mind's eye what was on that canvas.

I'd gone through my parents' music collections and ripped all their Broadway musical CDs. Then I'd started on opera. I'd never been a great fan of opera, but the aria that Allison had sung still rang in my ears and I needed to find out if there was more than that. I spent too much time trying to understand what was going on in the story if I listened to operas in English. German operas seemed harsh to me. But the French and Italian operas just took me away and dropped me in a different world. I didn't understand anything that was going on in them, and I didn't care.

I didn't spend long periods of time in my zone while I was painting. There's a surprising amount you can do without losing yourself, and my parents did want a coherent son home for a visit. By this time, I'd shown them photos of the mural and my paintings from the year. It's great to have a digital camera. I just load all the pictures on my computer and set up a slide show. Of course, Dad wanted me to transfer it all to his computer so they could show all their friends.

I also showed them the letter from Bob Bowers. It was the first time I'd shown it to anyone. Melody, Lissa, and Lexi all knew what was in it since they'd heard Jack read it to me, but it didn't feel right to share it with anyone else, at least not until I'd shown it to Mom and Dad.

Being back in Nebraska, though, had a damping effect on my attitude.

———⊲◆▷———

"YOU WOULD NOT believe what he pulled," Melody said as we held our nightly three-way chat. We'd also had enough text messages that I'd had to change my phone plan so I didn't get charged an arm and a leg. "He set me up on a blind date! We went out to dinner and Ricky, this boy I had a crush on in high school, came up to us in the restaurant to say hi out of the blue. Dad asked him to join us and then had a sudden mysterious phone call and said he had to leave. He asked Ricky if he'd mind taking me home. He left me stranded at Legal Sea Foods with a boy I hardly knew."

"I thought you said you had a crush on him," I said, laughing.

"From afar! He was a jock and I did not even speak to jocks in high school. But he does have beautiful eyes, and..." she sighed.

"So what happened?" Lissa asked.

"Oh we just talked over dinner and then I asked him to take me home. He starts in on this spiel about how he always thought I was the cutest in class and he was too shy to ask me out. Right. Like I believed him," Melody huffed.

"I was too shy to ask you out," I said. "You were my secret crush."

"Tony! You never noticed me."

"Did too! Promise."

"Oh, come on, you two. I want to know what happened. Did you do anything? Secret crush, there in your arms, beautiful eyes," Lissa sighed as if this wasn't our lover we were talking to.

"Well... um... he... we kissed. But I didn't like it. Too much. I told him not to call me again." Melody ended.

"Meddy, you know nobody's telling you not to have any fun while you are out there," I said. "We know you love us." I wasn't completely convinced that I meant what I said, but damn it, it was hard being separated from our lovers. I wouldn't mind a nice kiss about now.

We chatted on until Melody was yawning so often that we all said goodnight and went to sleep. I wondered as I drifted off why I wasn't as willing to let my lovers have other relationships as they were for me. I had to work on that.

―――――◁◆▷――――

I MET A couple friends for a burger and fries, and it seemed like we were in different worlds. I didn't mention my living arrangements and my girlfriends.

I spent a couple of hours a day at the local Y where I learned to play racquetball, but I didn't pick up any matches. I just went onto the court and beat myself silly, looking for the zone that was proving so elusive to me since I'd been back in Nebraska. My former instructor came by and complimented me on my progress, but I didn't feel like I was performing anywhere near my peak, even when Dad came over to play one day. I needed Lissa.

It seemed strange that no one ever asked me if I had a girlfriend, but I guess I was a little relieved. I just didn't think anyone here would understand—assuming anyone believed it. Classmates who knew me for years still thought I wasn't really attracted to girls. The fact was that I'd been so afraid of them I couldn't even talk to a girl.

All except one. My best friend was a girl. She was funny and outgoing and had tons of friends, but never a boyfriend. I was welcome to hang around whenever she was with a group, whether it was with boys or girls or both. But she didn't date any more than I did. My few attempts were bumbling at best.

As for Beth, it might have been her weight that kept her from dating. I don't know. She was just my friend and I didn't really care about whether she was overweight. That bubbling personality always brightened my day. So when Mom called me to the phone Friday afternoon, I was really pleased to hear it was Beth.

"Dumpling!" I exclaimed when I answered the phone. "You're back home."

"Hi, Pogo. I got back yesterday. I hear you're still painting."

"Oh, didn't you hear I'd become a jock? I spend all day pumping iron and doing crunches."

"Right. And I'm a cheerleader." We laughed, but her laugh sounded a little strained.

"So when are we getting together?" I asked. Man, it was so easy just to talk to her over the phone like the past year had never happened and we were still the skinny art boy and the bubbly fat smart girl in high school. Beth had a scholarship to Wellesley, where she was studying International Relations. Smart girl—did I mention that?

"Tonight. Donny Cavanaugh is having a 'welcome back to Nebraska' party for all the college kids home for the summer. I'm picking you up at six-thirty and we'll head for the farm."

"Six-thirty? It's already after five. Thanks for the warning. I need to… you know… wash my hair and stuff," I said. This time Beth's laugh was deep and genuine. It had been a long-standing joke that if one of us asked the other if he or she had a date we'd make up some lame-ass excuse for not being able to go out.

"You have your skinny ass on the porch waiting for my big red truck at six-thirty sharp or I'll drag you out by your ear," she said. "No wimping out tonight, Pogo. We have serious partying to do."

OKAY. I GUESS that's that. I didn't really have to wash my hair, but I did put on a clean pair of jeans and t-shirt. Then I spent the next hour on the phone with my girlfriends.

"Wellesley? Damn! I could have met her before she came home. It's only like twenty minutes from here," Melody said.

"Sounds to me like your high school crush wants to pick up where she wished things had been before graduation," Lissa laughed. "What is it about these Midwestern girls, Mel?"

"I don't know, but I want to be on the phone with you both when she rolls out of Tony's bed tomorrow morning."

"It's not like that, you guys," I said. I knew that. They knew that. But they were still teasing. God! I missed my sweethearts.

"I know, baby," Melody said. "But still. She was your best friend in high school and you haven't been very good about keeping up with people since you left. She might have all kinds of expectations, or at least hopes."

"I don't think so," I said. "But I'll be on guard."

"Don't be on guard," Lissa said, "but do be aware. I have absolutely no experience with this kind of thing because I didn't go to regular school after I was fifteen. I was on the road all the time and Jack had me tutored. But I still remember a cute boy that I was *so* in love with in ninth grade. I just know I'd go out of control if I met him now. At least if he was still as cute as he was eleven years ago."

"And you know what happened to me last weekend," Melody said. "As if setting me up with Ricky wasn't enough, I've been asked out by five different boys Dad gave my number to. And I did kiss Ricky."

"Hey. Kissing a high school crush is nothing to get bent out of shape over," I said. We'd talked about Melody's big adventure. The big kiss had done nothing for her and she'd let the guy know that he shouldn't call her again. We were just in a different world now that we had each other, no matter what old friends or infatuations we met up with.

"The thing is," Lissa said, "this is a time that we have away from each other and we shouldn't think of it as being a time of fear and testing. If it feels right, do it."

"Yeah," Melody confirmed. "But you might call and let us listen in. That could be fun!"

"You two are terrible. Here. I'm taking a picture out of our yearbook and sending it to you." I found Beth's photo in the yearbook and clicked my cell phone camera, then sent the image to my girlfriends. "Now you can fantasize about my evening to your heart's content," I laughed.

"Look at that smile!" Lissa said. "She has to have been the most popular girl in school."

"She was everybody's friend, but never dated more than a few times as far as I know," I answered. "It just wasn't the way we were in high school."

"She may have been uncomfortable with her self-image," Melody said. "I think she's sexy as hell."

"Oh, you think that about all girls," I said.

"True," Melody said. "Tony, just do what feels right to you and don't *not* do things because you feel guilty. We are not having any kind of relationship built on guilt."

"That goes for me, too," Lissa said. "It's hard enough being without you two. Don't add feeling bad because one of us might do something without the others. Just please always be honest with us."

"And just what kind of trouble are you getting into without us?" I asked. I already knew, of course. We'd been talking every day.

"Oh, just this cute little brunette who comes around to play with the boys. Sometimes she sleeps over. Once she even took a hot tub with me," Lissa said.

"Mmm," I said. "I think I need a minute just to think about that image."

"Yeah. And maybe have a smoke afterward," Melody said.

"Did you talk to her today?" Lissa asked.

"Yes," both Melody and I answered. Then we all broke up laughing. We all knew the truth. Even though we didn't talk as long to Kate, we all talked to her almost every day.

"God, I can't wait to get back home!"

"That goes for me, too," Melody said. "She made little kissy noises at me when we hung up today. I could almost feel those sensuous lips."

Kate hadn't been far from any of our thoughts since school let out. She was hanging around and visiting Lissa whenever she could. When Melody and Lissa and I talked, Kate was frequently the subject of our conversation and occasionally was on the line with us. Whenever my phone rang I found myself hoping it might be Kate. None of us knew where this would go, but we were all a little breathless thinking about it.

Kate was courting us.

Sixteen

A T SIX-THIRTY sharp, a bright red pickup truck came tearing down our driveway in a cloud of dust. Beth's Dad bought her the 4x4 for her eighteenth birthday. "Boys love girls in trucks," he'd said as he handed her the keys. We'd all laughed because she had to have the seat customized so she could reach the pedals and still see out the windshield. Beth barely topped five feet, but she loved that truck.

I stepped off the front porch and sauntered toward where she'd stopped, but I was still several feet away when her door opened and I saw her legs drop down below the door. I don't think I'd ever seen Beth's bare legs except maybe once when we all went swimming. She was strictly a blue jeans girl in high school. But these weren't the chubby little legs I remembered from that outing. Nor was the svelte, stacked babe that stepped around the truck door the "Dumpling" of my childhood.

"Beth?" I said. I knew I shouldn't gawk, but... "Wow!"

"So where's this hot jock I'm supposed to be dating?" she asked, posing by the door.

"I'd say he's still upstairs, but you'd make me go get him," I said. "Wow, Dumpling!" I stopped myself. "I can't really call you that anymore, can I?"

"Tony, you can call me the south end of a horse headed north if you want to. What I look like doesn't change who I am."

"I hope not!" I said. "But what you look like might give *some* guys a different idea."

"Really, Pogo? What kind of ideas does it give you?" she swished herself over to where I'd stopped and put her hands behind my neck. It was still a bit of a reach.

"Oh! I don't mean me, Dumpling! I just mean... well... shit... what do I mean?"

"I think you mean you were about to get in the truck," she growled.

"Yeah. Exactly." We turned and headed for the truck and Beth caught hold of my arm and squeezed it. Then she stopped and spun me toward her. She squeezed my bicep a little more and then poked me in the stomach. I saw it coming and tensed my gut, so she didn't sink in at all. She grabbed my shirttails and pulled it up to expose my stomach. Well, I have been working out for a while and Pilates does wonders for the abs.

"Jesus Christ, Pogo! You didn't really go and become a jock, did you?"

"Well, I do play," I said.

"Last time I heard, the only thing you played was racquetball."

"Yeah. Imagine my surprise to find out it was a sport," I chuckled. I pulled my shirt down and she pulled it back up to poke at my stomach again. Finally, she let the shirt fall back down.

"You got washboard abs from playing racquetball?"

"Well, not just. It was from all the training."

"Training for what?"

"Intercollegiate National Championships and the National Singles Championships," I said calmly. Well, hell. I was proud of it. This was the first real opportunity I'd had to brag about it.

"When?"

"I got back on Mothers' Day."

"Back?"

"From Chicago. Where the championships were played."

"Did you win?"

"No. But I played."

"No way."

"I've got it on video. It's on YouTube." Beth grabbed my arm and marched me right back toward the house.

"I suppose there's a Tony Ames Channel on YouTube now, right?" she snarled. I stopped and gasped. That thought hadn't crossed my mind.

"Geez! I hope not. Where are we going?"

"You're going to show me. Right now."

I took her into the family room where Dad had down-loaded my match against Karl onto our set-top box and I knew he'd shown it to a few other people who had come over. The TV was set to play it. Beth sat at the edge of the sofa watching the seven-point match.

"That's the national champion I'm playing," I filled her in. "His name's Karl Higgendorfer and he's a great guy."

"You played him in the tournament?"

"No. I did actually win a couple of matches in the tourna-ment. Karl challenged me to a match the day before the tour-nament began."

"The national champion challenged *you* to a pre-tourna-ment match-up." She looked at me when the finished the video. "What else?"

"A lot of things have changed since last year," I said. Before I could continue, though, she jumped up.

"Let's go," she commanded. She was dragging me out to the truck. "That bitch Ramona is going to be at this party and you had better have eyes for no one but me. Got it? I want every boy and every girl at the party to be pissed over what they missed out on. For both of us."

"Don't you want to, like… entice someone?" I asked. Shit, I thought she'd be ready to prey on all the people who'd dissed her in high school.

"Oh yeah," she smiled.

———————◄◆►———————

YOU'VE GOT TO understand a bit about country parties. It's not like going to somebody's apartment in the city and getting drunk on cheap wine or worse rum where you're confined to three rooms and a sofa. We party outside… on a farm… with woods, creeks, barns, sheds, bushes, and heavy implements. Donny had a volleyball net set up and by the time we got there, they were already picking up teams. Beth dragged me over and immediately declared that we were playing. Donny looked at her and his eyes got as big as saucers. He stammered.

"Yeah. Sure. You can be on my team."

Stoney, apparently the team captain for the opposition, looked daggers at Donny. I don't think he knew who either of us were. He pointed at me and said, "Yeah. You, over here."

I was headed that way when Beth grabbed my arm.

"Lose the shirt, stud," she said and proceeded to peel her own top off. She was wearing a bikini top under it and every male and most of the female eyes were riveted to it. Beth had lost a lot of weight the past year, but none of it came off her breasts. There was enough saliva being dripped on the ground to make it muddy. I stripped off my shirt and tensed my abs for

Beth's benefit, and *that* didn't go unnoticed, either. We grinned at each other and took our places.

I'm not a great volleyball player. But I *was* in great shape. So when other guys were sagging out and running for a beer, I was still returning serves and everyone discovered I had a wicked spike. My side lost, mostly because all the guys were so intent on Beth's boobs they missed every shot. When we headed toward our shirts, guys were mobbing Beth. I noticed the aforementioned Ramona headed toward me.

Ramona was every geek's nemesis. Cheerleader, beauty queen—or what passed for one in Nebraska—and a personality that was all about how she, and everyone else, looked. While neither Beth nor I were exactly geeks, we didn't fit in for other reasons. Beth was valedictorian and I was an artist. 'Nuf said. We were always fair game for Ramona's self-glorifying barbs. Her graduation day remark had offended nearly everyone. "Well, of course she's valedictorian. What else did she have to do?"

I caught Beth's eye and nodded my head toward the approaching bitch. She broke away from the guys who were complimenting her and was by my side before Ramona could reach me. Not bothering with her shirt, she grabbed my arm and spun me in the opposite direction.

"Come on," she said brightly. "After that workout, I need a drink!" We marched away from the descending Ramona and, by the time we reached the drinks, we were laughing our asses off.

———◁◆▷———

CONTRARY TO POPULAR opinion, hot, horny teenagers in the middle of the Bible belt don't just sneak into their bedrooms or the nearest hayloft and fuck. There are rituals to be observed, and if you drive a truck or a car without much backseat, there is a limitation to the places you can really go. But we have land. And our land has a lot of hiding places on it if you can figure out a way to get to it without drawing attention. So we have games. Like hide 'n' seek. Played with couples. You get the idea.

As soon as the game was called, Beth grabbed my hand and two beers and dragged me away. The thing is that the couple that's doing the seeking, can't go make out in the bushes until they find another couple. So they really look hard and most of us know all the good places to hide, even those of us who barely ever played. Cavanaugh's had plenty of places around the farm and the rule was you had to hide within the fence-lines. I had no idea where to go, but Beth apparently had a plan.

We made a stop at her truck and she opened the door. That turned on the dome light which I was sure was visible from where the seekers were counting out their time. Just in case they hadn't seen, she made a point of slamming the door shut as soon as she'd retrieved a blanket from behind the seat. Then instead of heading into the yard, she headed toward the road.

"Hey, we have to stay within the fence-line," I said naively.

"No. We have to *hide* within the fence-line," she corrected me. We headed out their property gate, took a right along the road and came back in the corn field next to the property, staying low since the corn was only a couple feet tall. When we'd circled all the way to the back fence-line, she hunched over and I followed her along the fence to a space beside the raspberry patch. No one ever went out there because the ground was hard and you never knew when you'd find an unexpected thorn. But armed with her heavy dark blanket, Beth headed straight for the patch, laid the blanket down next to it and then herself. When I'd lain down beside her, she flipped the blanket up and covered us, effectively blocking light from reflecting off our skin.

"Now," she said, "just lie here quietly and keep us covered."

"It's getting hot in here," I said. Actually that was true on multiple levels. The day had been plenty warm, and even though it was after eleven, it was still plenty hot out and the blanket was increasing the temperature. But Beth had planned this and it was her bikini-top clad skin pressed against mine that was making things hot, humid, and sticky. I was still a teen for another two-and-a-half months yet. I was acutely aware of the bare, sexy skin touching me, and even more aware of the lips that were suddenly pressing insistently against mine.

"We really have the last laugh on all of them, Pogo," Beth whispered against me. "None of them would have anything to do with us in high school, and now they are all wondering what they missed. And here we are, finding out."

"But Beth…" I started. She shut me up with another kiss and I let my lips part at the insistence of her tongue. Geez! I always liked Beth. She was my best pal. We did so much together, but…

Holy shit! She'd reached down and grabbed my cock through my shorts. *Damn! Shit! Fuck! No!* I broke the kiss and pushed her away, grabbing for her hand and pulling it up off my sudden erection.

"Tony, I saved myself for you. I want you to be the one," she whispered, pulling my hand to her breast.

"No, Beth," I said, pulling away. "I can't. Please."

"No! You're not really… that was all a rumor… please tell me you're not really gay."

"I'm *really not* gay," I said.

"Then it's okay?" she asked pleadingly.

"No," I said. "Girlfriend."

Beth didn't scream at me. Didn't hit me. Didn't react anything like I thought would be logical—but what do I really know about girls? She buried her head against my chest, wrapped her arms around me, and quietly sobbed against me.

What could I do? I held her. I petted her hair. She was my best friend for years, sometimes the only kid at school I could call a friend. And I'd just hurt her. I wept as well.

WE LEFT THE party about midnight. We'd never been found. We just stayed under the blanket whispering together. When we left and headed past the bonfire, people just stared at the two of us, holding hands and carrying a dark blanket to the bright red pick-up. We didn't say goodbye to anyone.

Beth drove up to my house and got out of the truck to walk up with me. I hugged her at the door. When I opened it she started to come in with me.

"Um… Beth, I'm going to go to bed now. Alone." She shook her head at me.

"I want to see."

"See what?"

"Her picture. You must have pictures of her." Oh boy. *Interestinger and interestinger, said Alice.* I hadn't told anyone other than my parents what my real arrangement was. But Beth was my best friend in high school. I figured I owed her this.

"Okay. Come on."

We walked up the old farmhouse stairs, which creaked unmercifully. Sure enough, before we got to my door my parents' bedroom door opened and Mom stepped out into the hall.

"Is that you, Tony?" she asked. Well, unless Dad was out partying someplace, I'm the only one she would expect to be coming home at this hour, right?

"Yeah, Mom. You remember Beth, right?"

"Of course. Oh Beth, you look beautiful. Please try to be quiet," Mom said. "We just got to sleep."

"I'm going to make a phone call, Mom," I said. "So I'll close my door."

"Of course you will," she smiled.

Mom retreated to her room and I led Beth into mine. Once the door was shut, I pulled out my cell phone, but before I could dial, Beth had gone straight to my easel and pulled the cover off the painting.

Seventeen

"**O**H MY god!" she gasped. She stood studying the painting. "Oh my god," she repeated. She moved back from the painting and then moved forward again.

"Oh my god." She sat on the foot of my bed. "She's crying for you. God, Tony, why is your girlfriend crying for you. She's begging you. Oh my god." Tears ran from Beth's eyes.

"Beth. Hey Dumpling," I said as I stroked her shoulder. "That isn't my girlfriend...exactly."

"Exactly? What does that mean? Wait!" Beth hadn't stopped looking at the painting since she sat down. I'd seen her look at my paintings before and she was looking for what I'd hidden. I often put shapes in the leaves of a landscape or hid treasures among the rocks I painted and Beth had become an expert at finding the hidden images. I'd been surprised that, as far as I knew, no one had found the shadowy figure in the doorway of the Rhapsody painting during the gala. I didn't do it as much anymore, but I knew she'd spot what I'd put in the painting of Allison. "They're watching her. No. They're watching you and her. They love her. They love you both. Tony, what happened?"

"It's not a tragedy," I reassured her. She could see the images of Lissa and Melody I'd painted into the shadows. They were always there when Allison and I were together. I don't know if Allison could see them, but everywhere I looked I saw my lovers. I'd painted them into the picture because they were as much a part of it as Allison was. "I'm going to call them now, so please be patient while I get them on the line."

"Them? You have more than one girlfriend, Tony?"

"Hey, I've changed a lot, but I'm still your Pogo," I said, "just like you're my Dumpling." I dialed Melody first and her sleepy voice answered on the third ring.

"'Lo?"

"Hi, darling. I know it's late, but I need to get you and Liss on the line and introduce you to someone."

"It's one o'clock in the morning," Melody said. Then she seemed to spring awake. "Is *she* with you?"

"Just be patient, Meddy," I said. "I'm going to put you on hold and dial Lissa now." I did and Lissa was considerably more awake.

"Hello, Lover," she said. "Kate and I are sitting on the deck watching the stars. Are you home from your party?"

"Hi, sweetheart," I said. "Yeah. Let me connect Melody. I want to introduce you to someone." I cut her squeal off before I connected to Melody. When I was sure I had them both I put them on speaker so Beth could hear and I sat beside her.

"Okay," I started. "Lissa and Melody, I want you to meet my best friend from high school, Beth Carpenter. Beth, these are my girlfriends, Lissa and Melody."

"Hi, Beth!" Melody shouted. "We saw your picture. Wish we were there with you."

"Um… Hi… I guess," Beth said.

"Oh yeah, I'm Melody, out in Boston," she said.

"And I'm Lissa, back in Seattle," Lissa added. "It's nice to meet you, Beth."

"It's nice to meet you, too," Beth said. "Are you really Tony's girlfriends?"

"Sure are," Lissa said.

"Beth, we're all in love with each other," I explained.

"You always were an odd one, Pogo," she answered.

"Who's Pogo?" Melody asked.

"It's a nickname. We grew up calling each other Pogo and Dumpling," Beth said. "You two are in the background of the picture, did you know that?"

"What picture?" Lissa asked.

"Well, I was saving it as a surprise," I said. "I've been working on an oil painting of Allie. And yes, the two of you are benevolently watching over her."

"That's not it, Pogo," Beth broke in. "It's not benevolence. I can see the love in their eyes. How do you do it?"

"Do you mean how do we love each other?" Lissa asked. "It's just so easy."

"Do you know anything about art, Beth?"

"Wait. Who is that?"

"Oh, sorry. I'm Kate."

"Are you a girlfriend?" There was some giggling on the other end of the line.

"Not exactly," I explained. "I'm not sure any of us have figured out what Kate is." I heard a raspberry being blown. "Kate, you know you're going to hear stuff that's… you know… intimate, right?"

"Well, if Beth can listen, can't I?"

"Of course you can, Kitten," I said. "As long as you know. Now what were you saying?"

"Did you call me Kitten?"

"I'm sorry, Kate."

"Don't be sorry! I love it! I'm a Kitty Kate."

"Um… yeah." I heard the definite sound of a kiss over the phone and as far as I knew, Lissa and Kate were the only others who were together.

"Okay, so Beth," Kate said. "Have you ever seen a triptych?"

"That's one of those three panel paintings, right?" Beth asked.

"That's right. Well, you have to think of Tony and Lissa and Melody like a triptych. Each panel is a complete painting in itself. But if you don't see all three panels together, you never really see the whole picture," Kate explained.

"But you all know about Allie in this painting?" Beth asked.

"Yes," Lissa answered. "Allie is dear to all of us. I can't wait to see the painting. Is she crying?"

"Yes. She has her hand held out to him and it's like she's just opening herself, so vulnerable, so… oh, god. It's the most beautiful thing I've ever seen."

"You haven't seen what else Tony has painted this year," Melody said softly. "We've all modeled for him. I've seen your picture. You should model for him, too."

"About that," I broke in. "I think I'd better send you a new picture." I had Beth stand up and snapped a picture of her. We'd never stopped to pick up our shirts at the volleyball pit. I hit send and in a minute I heard Melody exclaim, "Wow! What a fox!" Beth blushed.

"I want to see pictures of you!" Beth said. I woke up my laptop and launched my "girlfriend" slide show, pointing out which one was Lissa, which Melody, the two boys, Kate, Allie, and so on. I had pictures of everyone and about half of them were nudes. The pictures of my paintings were in the mix and Beth was exclaiming over them.

Finally, I heard Lissa over the phone.

"Lover," Lissa said, "it's time for some girl talk. Just leave the phone with Beth and go get yourself some nice warm milk or something, okay?" I could hear the tease in her voice. But I wanted to make absolutely clear that both Kate and Beth heard what I had to say next.

"Lissa, I love you. Good night, darling. Melody, I love you. I'll talk to you in the morning, okay? Oh. And Kate, I think about you a lot. You know how special you are to us, right?"

"Goodnight, Tony," Kate said. "I know."

"Goodnight, love."

"Sweet dreams, sweetheart."

I handed the phone to Beth and left the room.

———◁◆▷———

I WAS NODDING off at the kitchen table when Beth came into the room. It was nearly two in the morning. I stood up to greet her in that kind of half-awake and half dreaming state. Beth handed me the phone and said, "Sorry, the battery's dead."

Then she kissed me.

All through school and growing up, I'd had… maybe… a dozen kisses ranging from experimental pecks to my first, second, and last, French kiss before leaving for college—the first one an experimental disaster between Beth and me. But this kiss was so full of friendship and love that I couldn't help but respond. I closed my eyes and just let myself be lost in the experience. I was aware that my hand stroked up and down her back and, as if it had a mind of its own, it had glided to the front to cup her huge breast.

Beth broke our kiss, but held my hand against her breast for a minute. She looked up at me and met my eyes.

"I've decided to save myself a little longer," she said. "But someday soon, Pogo, you're going to paint me."

She pulled away from me and I watched her red pick-up drive away before I dragged myself to bed and collapsed.

Eighteen

I **STOOD** in the doorway, staring again at the little twin bed in the room I'd grown up in—Allison's picture no longer draped. I'd been 'home' for more a month and I wasn't sure how I could bear to go into this room again. I had to talk to Mom and Dad today about going back to Seattle. And somehow I had to get Melody there with us.

Mom and Dad had come in to see the painting when I told them about the unusual night I had with Beth. Dad had given me a hug. Not just a squeeze or a man-hug, but an all-out bear hug that threatened to crack my ribs.

"It's so much better than seeing photographs of your work," Mom said. She walked up to it and without touching it traced the outline of the shadow figures with her finger. "You know we are always here for you, too, Tony," she said as she left the room.

Saturday, she and Dad had a whispered conference in the kitchen and then Dad left for the rest of the day. When he came back in time for dinner, he announced that we were going camping and asked me to get the gear ready first thing Sunday morning. He and Mom were going into Omaha to pick up supplies. *Damn it!* I'd talk to them while we were traveling.

I spent a long time on the phone with my lovers Saturday night. Crying.

SUNDAY MORNING, I dutifully got out the tents, sleeping bags, portable grill, equipment, and water jugs. Once the sleeping bags were opened and hung on the line in the sun to air out, I went inside and showered, returning to the cave of my room. I wanted to spend some time with Mom and Dad, sure, but I really missed Melody and Lissa. Melody had had a rough weekend, too, and we'd talked much of the night with Lissa. Most of the time one or more of us was crying. Somehow, I had to get my family back together.

I heard the car pull in the drive, telling me Mom and Dad were back. I was going to have to tell them I couldn't go on this trip. I needed to get my family back together. I'd empty my savings and fly to Boston, pick up Melody and fly to Seattle. It was the only way.

"Tony!" Dad called from downstairs. "Tony! Did you get the gear all prepared?"

"Yeah, Dad," I said coming downstairs. "Two tents, air mattresses, sleeping bags, grill, tarps, ropes, canteens, mess kits. Everything is there and aired out. I just need to roll the sleeping bags back up and stuff them in their bags. But Dad…"

"How much equipment do you think you'll need for a week on the road with your two ladies?" Dad cut me off. I looked at him, not quite comprehending what he was asking. "Come on, son. Let me show you something."

We walked out the front door and there was a cherry red Ford Escape sitting in the drive. *When did Dad get that?* I wondered.

"This is something I'd planned for next summer to celebrate your twenty-first birthday, Tony. But it seems that the timetable has moved up. A family man needs a family car. This gets good mileage—in fact, better than the later models—has comfortable seating for five, and room for cargo. It gets thirty miles a gallon on the highway, so it shouldn't cost too much to operate," Dad said leading me out to the car. I could tell by the license plates that it wasn't new, but it looked to be mint condition. He handed me the keys.

"Dad?" I said. I couldn't believe what I thought he was telling me.

"It comes with a year's insurance paid and a full tank of gas. There's a prepaid fuel card in the glove box with a thousand-dollar credit on it," Dad said. "Son, your family needs you. Your mom and I have talked to Lexi and Melody is stressed out. Lissa says even the boys want to know when you are coming home. I know you talk to them, but Melody needs you to take her home to your family. Pack up the camping gear you need. Mom's getting food ready for the cooler. We're not trying to get rid of you and we expect you to stop here on your way back west, but if you can get your butt in gear, you could be on the road at seven tomorrow morning."

I was overwhelmed. I didn't know what to say or how to tell my dad how much I loved him. I just wrapped him up in a big hug and danced around the yard. Next thing I knew, Mom was in the dance, too, as I thanked them and hollered out my happiness.

I knew just what I needed to do next. I pulled out my cell and called Lissa.

"Hi, baby, I miss you," she said as soon as she got on the line. "Is Melody on, too?"

"No, Lissa," I said. "This is just between you and me."

"Tony?"

"Can you get away for that week of vacation you mentioned?"

"I'm pretty flexible. You know my work schedule. If I've got my laptop I just need to check in each day. Tony, what's up?"

I explained what my folks had done and inside of five minutes I could hear Lissa screaming "Yes! Yes! Yes!" through the phone. When she was off the line, I thought about all the times we'd all been together, and the times that Melody had done something special for me that helped me through school and life. I knew I'd get a phone call buzzing back at me in minutes, but I tapped out a text message for Melody.

"Darling, pack everything. Will be there on Wednesday to take you home."

———◁◆▷———

WHEN I LEFT in my new car on Monday morning, I think I could have driven straight through to Boston without stopping. Dad made me promise not to drive more than six hundred miles or ten hours in a day, though. He said he wanted me to be with my family, not to have them gathered at my gravesite. Honestly, though, stopping in the parking lot at Walmart in Elkhart, Indiana for the night when it was only five p.m. was a pain. I didn't bother trying to camp on the way out. I just cranked the passenger seat back and slept. Of course, the fact that the store was open 24 hours meant that people were driving in and out of the parking lot all night long, and three huge campers pulled up near me to spend the night as well.

I was out of there at six the next morning, but the day went a lot slower. I kept having to pull off to get coffee and burgers to keep me fueled. It was no farther to Syracuse, New York than I drove on Monday, but I didn't pull in until seven that night. Half the time I was driving, I had my phone connected to the

Bluetooth system in the car and was talking to my loves. They kept me awake, at least. I know that technically it took more than the ten hours of allotted drive time, but when I stopped, I knew I was within range of Boston and what would be my trickiest day.

Melody didn't live in Boston proper, though we always referred to it that way, but rather in the historic town of Lexington. At three in the afternoon, I drove right past her little town and through the craziness of Boston to Logan International Airport. I was never so happy in my life to see Lissa swinging a backpack over her shoulder and rushing off the curb to climb into my car. She kissed me so hard and so long that the next car in line at the curb started blasting its horn to get me to hurry up and move.

Now we had a little surprise for Melody.

It doesn't seem to make any difference what time you go through Boston; it's rush hour. It took nearly an hour and about a dozen wrong turns to navigate the twenty-five miles to Melody's house. She was waiting for me and came running out the door as soon as I pulled into her driveway. Lissa and I threw our carefully orchestrated surprise to the wind and just both jumped out of the car to rush our girlfriend. When Melody saw it was both of us she stopped running and began jumping in place screaming. The girl gets a little emotional.

--------◅◆▻--------

IT WAS FIVE o'clock when people started arriving. Supposedly, they were just there to help Melody pack. Well, even with getting her loom broken down and packed, it only took about an hour to cart her stuff out to the car and fill it to the gills. We kept the camping gear accessible and a seat for each of us, but the rest of the car was jammed. Lexi opened the garage and I pulled in beside her Corolla so the Escape wouldn't be on the street overnight. Then everyone headed for the backyard where a neighbor had the grill working and hot dogs and burgers on it. It turned out that Melody had invited several friends, as had Lexi, to meet her boyfriend and girlfriend. Melody was leaving town with a splash.

She and Lissa disappeared for a few minutes at which time a tall, thin guy with sandy hair and the darkest green eyes I'd ever seen on a man walked up to me. He held out his hand and when I took it, he squeezed just a little harder than necessary. I didn't try to compete; I just looked at him while he introduced himself.

"I'm Ricky Barlowe," he said. "Congratulations on making the best catch in Lexington." I smiled at him and said thanks, but he wasn't finished with me. "Look, I don't know how this thing of yours works, but Melody is special and I will hurt anyone who hurts her." He was looking right into my eyes and still gripping my hand tight enough to let me know he meant business. It was just at the soft edge of being painful.

"Ricky," I said, "we all need our friends. But Melody and Lissa are more than that to me. They're my family. They are strong, independent women and don't need anyone to come to their aid. That includes guys who kissed my girlfriend a couple weeks ago." He was really taken aback and let go of my hand. He apparently didn't think Melody would tell me that they'd kissed.

"Look, I didn't mean... I didn't know at the time..." All shook up.

"Hey," I said. "From what I hear, she enjoyed it. But if there's ever anything else she needs from you, she has your number."

We were interrupted at that point by Melody and Lissa returning and Ricky backed away. I was pretty sure he'd been filled with a lot of crap from Mr. Anderson. But the girls had something on their mind and dragged me over to Lexi. Lexi in turn, called for everyone's attention. Then she made the formal introduction of Lissa and me. She made sure to let everyone know that Melody was girlfriend to both of us and was moving out west to be with us. Then she turned it over to Melody.

"A lot of you have noticed the necklaces Lissa and I are wearing. Tony surprised us in Chicago with them, but we didn't have anything for him. Well, in the meantime, our present for him has arrived and you can all witness it." She took my left hand in hers and Lissa held out a length of silver chain.

"I get to go first again," Lissa whispered, "so I suppose tonight…" She giggled and then spoke up so everyone could hear. "Tony, this isn't quite as intimate a setting as when you gave us our jewelry, but we want everyone to know we love you. You've shown me so much about life and love since we met. You've been my friend, confidante, racquetball partner, and lover. You've been friend to my children and boyfriend to me. You introduced me to the sweetest girl I've ever met, and you showed me what it means to be looked at with love. I love you, darling." With that she laid the bracelet across my wrist where Melody held it in place while Lissa kissed me.

"Darling Tony," Melody said when Lissa and I had broken our kiss. "All year you were a shining light that I thought was out of reach. Then one day I got up the courage to ask you out, since it was obvious that you weren't going to do it." Everybody laughed. "Our dates were unconventional. We spent hours lying nude in front of each other under the guise of modeling for our art." Now everyone was laughing so much she had to pause to go on. "You introduced me to the woman we love and you let us see ourselves through your eyes. The connection and love swept me away. I love you." She finished fastening the bracelet on my wrist and gave me a passionate kiss. But the public ceremony wasn't finished.

Melody pulled Lissa's hand over to join ours. "You both let me grow and discover love more deeply than I'd ever imagined possible. I love you, Lissa."

"When I was sure I could never be what you wanted," Lissa picked up, "you wouldn't let go. You pulled this sinking ship to the surface and saved me. I love you, Melody."

Everyone had been told that we were definitely all three together, but there is nothing like a really hot kiss between two beautiful women to cause a collective gasp from onlookers. And when I joined the kiss, it quickly became obvious to them that the onlookers were no longer needed. People began to leave soon after. Everyone there stopped to wish us well and a safe trip home.

When Ricky came up he shook our hands—less aggressively this time—and also wished us luck. He was a little in awe as he looked from Melody to me to Lissa, but he was practically knocked off his feet when Lissa reached up and planted a good kiss on him.

"I know you were wondering," Lissa giggled. Ricky's eyes shot open and he gave me a nervous look, afraid, perhaps, that I'd be mad that he'd now kissed both my girlfriends. I intentionally misinterpreted his look.

"Don't look at me like that," I said lightly. "To me AC/DC is strictly a band." Ricky's mouth was still hanging open all the way out the door.

LEXI MADE NO objections to the three of us sleeping together and when we woke in the morning, we were happy and at least partially sated. It seemed like so long since we'd been together and our bodies craved the drug of each other.

Our noses told us bacon was frying downstairs and we showered, dressed, and were in the kitchen in record time for three naked horny lovers. Lexi had made us Mickey Mouse pancakes, eggs, and bacon and we washed it all down with pretty darn good coffee—a rarity for the Boston area, I'd found. It was about ten in the morning before we finally convinced Lexi that we had to get going. My folks were expecting us for the Fourth of July barbecue and I guessed it might take longer for the return trip than it had coming out. We went to the garage and Lexi opened the garage door.

Harold Anderson was standing in the middle of the drive.

He looked drawn and not nearly as pompous as he'd acted in Chicago. He was wearing a pair of chinos and a polo shirt. I hadn't seen him since the night Melody told him to go back to Boston. I knew she'd talked to him during her time home—after all, it was Harold who had set Melody up with Ricky—but I wasn't sure where their relationship was.

Leave it to Melody to just do the right thing. She marched down the drive toward her dad and flung her arms around him. Lissa and I hung back a little, but neither of us could let her get too far away.

"Thank you for coming to see me off, Daddy. I do love you, you know."

"Melody, baby, please don't ever think that your daddy doesn't love you. I'm sorry I've been hard to get along with and that… everything," he finished. There were tears in his eyes. "A father should walk his little girl down the aisle," he said, softly.

He pulled her right hand to his left arm and walked Melody toward Lissa and me. He held her hand and reached for ours, which we gave him. He held our three hands together between his and looked at each of us long and hard as if it were the last time he'd ever see us.

"Drive carefully," he said as a way of blessing. Then he turned away and we saw him get in his car and drive off.

We were on the road and heading west—facing home. Melody and Lissa were giggling and by the time I hit I-90, they were leaning over the seats kissing with loud rock music on the radio.

I pulled over at the tollbooth, stopped the car, and turned off the radio.

"Uh-oh," Melody sang. "We're in trou-ble."

"My darling lovers," I said. "There is one rule of the road that is absolute. No sex and no sex play while the car is running. As my dad told me, I want my family together, but I don't want them gathered at a gravesite." They could see that I was serious. They both reached for me and kissed my cheeks—Lissa from her position as first shotgun and Melody from the rear seat.

"However," I said, smiling, "there's a campground about 130 miles west of here… and we have a tent."

I put the car in gear and we headed west.

Nineteen

SUNDAY AFTERNOON, I was getting a little anxious. After a weeklong, 3,000-mile roundtrip to Boston, I was bringing my girlfriends—my family—home to my parents' house in Nebraska. I pointed out sights to them as we entered Nebraska. From the time we turned west on U.S. 30, I was like a three-year-old at the steering wheel, even pointing at the horses and cows in the field.

"There's where I went to high school," I said. "Man, it's changed already. Big renovation this year."

"Aw, that's sweet. I didn't show you my high school back in Lexington," Melody said.

"We were in a hurry to get you out of town!" Lissa said. "But we'll go back and you can show us around like tourists. Maybe at Christmas."

"Oh look," I said. I'd driven around the streets of Fremont acting like I was just cruising for the benefit of my girlfriends. My real goal was in sight now. "There's the YMCA. You'll love it there. It's where I learned to play racquetball. Three courts."

Lissa and Melody dutifully looked out the window and I plunged ahead.

"I know… Let's get a game in tomorrow morning, Lissa. I bet half the town would show up to see us play."

"Don't embarrass your girlfriend," Lissa scowled. *Uh-oh.*

"I'm sorry. Really. I couldn't stop him," I whined. Yeah, Melody doesn't have a corner on the whining market. I'm pretty good at it.

"Stop who? What?" Melody asked.

"Tony?"

"Dad," I said. "He's so excited to have you here to visit he arranged to have a court for us tomorrow morning for a kind of local exhibition."

I pulled into the Y parking lot and got out of the car, motioning the girls to join me as I approached the front doors. The Y closed early on Sunday afternoon, so they were locked up. Plastered against the glass of the door, though was a big poster that Dad had made up at Kinko's. The pictures were what he'd managed to download from the Internet.

"U.S. Women's Open Champion Lissa 'The Ice Queen' Grant vs. National Intercollegiate bronze medalist Tony 'Tornado Alley' Ames in an Independence Day Exhibition Match..." Lissa read from the poster. "Oh, Tony."

"Really, I couldn't," I complained.

"You are so going to get spanked," Lissa threatened.

"Hey! What do I have to do to get spanked?" Melody asked. We both looked at her and broke out laughing.

"Just get naked," I suggested before I thought about what I was saying.

Melody pulled her t-shirt over her head and went for her bra.

"Okay."

"No, no, no, no!" I said, "Sweetie, this is Nebraska!"

I rushed her to the car and got her inside as Lissa followed laughing at us.

"What would Saul and Deborah think?" she asked as she climbed in the front seat.

"Oh yeah," Melody sighed. "They'd want to watch, wouldn't they?"

"You, girl, might look and sound innocent, but you are just plain born evil," I laughed as we pulled away from the Y. I was relieved to see her smirk at me and pull her t-shirt back on. Rule one: No sex play when the car is running. It was only about ten minutes before we were out of town and I'd turned on the county road where we lived.

"It's so beautiful out here," Lissa said. "So peaceful."

"What's that?" Melody asked, pointing out the front window toward the west. The sun was in my eyes, so I wasn't too sure what she was pointing at.

"Well," I ventured, "I'm not sure if we're looking due west or slightly southwest. I think it's Wyoming, but it might be Colorado."

They were only three or four hundred miles away, and it was pretty much flat from here to there. That got me a well-deserved smack in the shoulder from two directions, but I didn't care because I was turning into our driveway.

"Tony, it's beautiful!" Melody exclaimed when she saw that we were at my folks' house.

"The pictures don't do it justice," Lissa added.

"What can I say? They're only photographs."

"You should paint it."

"Maybe I will one day."

Before we got out of the car the screen door banged on the porch and Mom and Dad were rushing to meet us. They had us wrapped up in so many hugs and kisses that we were never sure who was welcoming whom. Now that I had my family with me, it was sure good to be back.

Dad, of course, had already reached the car to try to grab suitcases or backpacks. I saw him just standing by the open door and went to join him. I pulled out Lissa's and my backpacks and Melody's small suitcase. Dad was still looking inside the car.

"I should have bought you a bigger car," he said.

"Everything fits, Dad," I answered.

"Yes, but what about *your* things?" Oh man! The car was packed as full as we could get it with Melody's things and nothing of mine was in it except the camping equipment. "I think we'll go down to U-Haul on Tuesday and see if we can get a small trailer," Dad continued. "You'll have to be careful because it won't drive the same when you're towing. Not as good gas mileage either, but… You *are* moving back to Seattle, aren't you?"

"Yes. Of course, Dad. Why would you even ask?"

"Well, you just got a fat envelope from Lincoln yesterday and it looks a lot like your acceptance packet did last year."

So much had changed since I applied to transfer to the University of Nebraska over the winter break, I couldn't even imagine going there now. I had a life in Seattle. Six months ago—just six months—I didn't. I looked at the two women who were my life as they continued to hug and chat with Mom.

"I hope you weren't planning on me moving back," I said to Dad. He joined me as we moved luggage toward the house.

"I'd have you committed if you did, son."

We went into the house through the kitchen and the girls oohed and aahed over the smells coming from the stove. Mom assured them that some of what they smelled—like the four big pies that were cooling on the counter—was for the barbecue tomorrow.

"Tony, take the girls' bags right on up to the guest room," Mom said.

"Mom…"

"Tony," she said. That look… I swear it's stopped trains. I took the bags up to the guest room with Dad trailing behind me.

"Uh… that one's mine," I said to Dad as he set my backpack down in the guest room.

"Mmmhmm."

"But…" I looked at the queen-sized bed in the guest room and thought about the twin in my room, comprehension beginning to dawn. "Oh."

I was back down in the kitchen when I heard the sound of tires on the gravel outside sliding to a stop. I looked out the door at the plume of dust that was still settling behind the red pickup. Mom was out the door before me, though, and was waving a wooden spoon in her hand scolding our visitor. The girls followed me out the door.

"Elizabeth Ann! Don't you come tearing in our drive like a hellion. There could have been children playing out there!"

"Oh my god! I'm sorry! I didn't think. Did you bring your kids?" she asked looking at me. I shook my head.

"But there could have been," Mom persisted.

"Yes'm," Beth said contritely. Then she looked back at me, and, satisfied that she'd been properly humble with Mom, came running up the steps to me. "Pogo!"

"Hi, Dumpling," I said. "I want you to meet…"

I never got the rest of the words out of my mouth. Beth dropped me like a hot potato and rushed to Melody and Lissa. They stood for a split second looking at each other and then fell into a hug that looked like they were long-lost friends who couldn't believe they'd found each other.

"You. Are. So. Beautiful!"

Well, that's the gist of what was said. I couldn't separate out which of the three girls was shouting it the loudest. I guessed that probably my presence was no longer required so I went inside with Mom. She handed me a stack of plates to set the table.

"Is it okay if Beth stays for dinner?" I asked.

"She's practically been camped out here all day waiting for you," Mom said. "If you don't set her a plate, she'll eat off yours."

"So, Lissa," Dad said as we ate Mom's incredible pot roast, "a few friends and I were wondering if you and Tony would give us a racquetball exhibition tomorrow morning. The Y is only open till noon on the Fourth and we have the barbecue in the afternoon, but it would mean a lot if you would show us how the game is supposed to be played."

"Sure, Saul," Lissa said. "Anything for you." I rolled my eyes. "I hope no one considers Tony too much of a local hero, though," she continued, "because I'm going to spank his butt on the court tomorrow."

I swear I heard Beth moan. I just hoped Lissa meant she was going to beat me at racquetball.

"They're so beautiful, Pogo," Beth said as I walked her out to her truck after she said goodnight to everyone. "And so nice!" We'd been sitting in the family room for the past two hours. It seemed that everyone had a favorite embarrass Tony story or ten that had to be told to girlfriends, best friends, and parents.

"I think so, too," I said. "Dumpling, I know you had a different kind of summer planned, but…"

"It was silly, Pogo. Forget about it. But…"

"What?"

"Could you still paint me? I've got an idea."

She laid out the basics of her plan and I had to admit it was good. This was going to be a very good visit to Nebraska.

————◁◆▷————

"Focus!"

How many times had I heard that in the past three months? I'd let my mind wander to the crowd of thirty or forty people outside the back glass of the court and another of Lissa's kill-shots had just sailed past me. *Don't embarrass your girlfriend,* I reminded myself. If I didn't play like I meant it, Lissa would be very upset. She might, indeed, spank my butt on the racquetball court, but not if I wasn't playing for real. I dropped the next shot just below her racquet and took over the serve.

As soon as my hand closed around the smooth blue surface of the ball, something inside me clicked. I stroked the rubber ball with my thumb, thinking of all the great games I'd had this spring and especially of the one with Karl at National Singles. *Just see where the ball will be,* I thought. *Forget about the walls.* I smiled and looked over my shoulder at Lissa to make sure she was ready as I walked into the server's lane. She saw it and smiled. *Now let's play racquetball.*

It really wasn't fair. She was playing on an unfamiliar court with borrowed equipment—my spares. I'd given her five points before I'd gotten my head in the game. But now we were playing at the level we were both capable of. I gained three of the five points back before the game was over. We took five and went right back at it like we'd never stopped.

When you are playing racquetball and are truly in the game, time stops. The world stops. There's just where the ball is going to be. I no longer saw Lissa on the court, but just the source of the ball's trajectory. Every muscle ripple in her shoulders and legs keyed into what I was going to do next; where I was going to be; how I was going to hit the ball. When a player is in that zone, he's unbeatable.

Unless his opponent is in the same zone.

When I had time to think about it later, I realized that Lissa had stepped up a level in her game. She'd entered the zone she'd asked me to teach her. It was a forty-minute game and she took me by one point.

We opened the door of the court to stagger out, with our arms wrapped around each other and applause from the gathered crowd.

"Yay, Lover!" Melody was shouting. Nice safe cheer. She was covered on all sides, though I could see a couple of people give her a strange look.

We were drenched in sweat and I couldn't think of anything but a shower and a hot tub before the club closed. I had to introduce Lissa and Melody to a dozen people, though, including my art teacher, my racquetball instructor, half a dozen high school friends, and several of my dad's friends. Most, we'd see again in the afternoon, but everyone wanted to say hi and how much they'd enjoyed the game. The last person I expected to see was Rev. Larkin. He was the Lutheran minister in town about ten years ago, but he'd moved away to a big church in Omaha before I was in junior high.

"Did you come all the way out here from Omaha?" I asked, shaking his hand.

"Oh no. I moved back here when I retired at the first of the year. I think the Synod had enough of my heresies and put me out to pasture, but when I actually had a choice of where I wanted to live, Fremont was the place. And these are?" he asked.

"Sorry!" I said. "These are my girlfriends, Lissa and Melody." Rev. Larkin didn't bat an eye.

"It's a pleasure to meet you," he said. "I hope we'll have a chance to chat at the barbecue this afternoon. I'm glad you are keeping Tony in line."

"We do our best," Lissa said.

"It takes both of us, though," Melody added.

Okay. I was a little embarrassed. But you know what? I was fucking proud, too. I was never religious and didn't go to church more than the other CEOs—that's Christmas and Easter Only—but Rev. Larkin was a good guy and I was proud that I'd introduced him to my girlfriends without stumbling over it or being embarrassed. And he just accepted it. I hugged both girls to me and said that we'd see him this afternoon. Then we headed to the showers while we could.

Twenty

MOM'S IDEA of a little Fourth of July barbecue amounted to about thirty people gathered in our backyard gabbing and eating for six hours. Many of the people who were watching the game in the morning were also at the barbecue. In addition to ribs, burgers, and dogs on the grill, Mom had baked apple, cherry, and strawberry/rhubarb pies. Everyone who came brought food, too. It was a Midwestern spread that you can only dream about in Seattle. Baked beans, potato salad, deviled eggs, macaroni and cheese, cobblers, pies, a cake, chips, coleslaw... you name it. There was even the requisite green Jell-O salad with flecks of shredded carrot in it. By four o'clock, the younger kids were all gathered around the ice cream makers, cranking the handle and stealing bits of rock salt to eat like candy. There were plenty of soft drinks and beer for the adults in ice chests, and even a bottle of wine or two. Of course, there was watermelon. You'd think all we had to do all day was eat.

Well... yeah.

My girlfriends were in high demand and Beth stood guard around them so the few classmates who were at the gathering understood that they were strictly off-limits. Of course, we all had to show our jewelry to everyone. It didn't take long for people to understand what the triple-hearts on their necklaces meant. Folks just kind of nodded their heads and commented about how different things were these days.

———◁◆▷———

WE ALL HAD dishes of ice cream—I love that kind where Beth's mom freezes Heath Bars and then shatters them to toss into the cream before it's frozen—and were sitting in lawn chairs under the shade of the huge elm tree in our backyard. Rev. Larkin came to sit beside us. He also examined the necklaces and then looked at the Celtic heart bracelet that I wore. It has a trefoil woven through the heart.

"I was surprised when you said you'd retired," I said. "I never think of you as being any older than my folks."

"Well, Tony, church politics are as divisive as national politics. The church is divided over the same issues and is still fighting battles that were resolved in the sixties. I just had enough of it. I wanted to return to a place out here where people were just people. I got a part-time job with the Chamber of Commerce."

"From what Deborah told me, it sounds like you were a little controversial," Lissa said.

"Oh, the fact that I was arrested a couple of times in demonstrations in favor of gay marriage and economic equality might have shaped that opinion," Rev. Larkin laughed. "If I hadn't volunteered to retire, I suspect I'd have been encouraged."

"I think it's great that you took a stand," I said. "I've never forgotten what you did for me."

Neither Melody nor Lissa had heard the story, so I told them about the day I disappeared to draw by the creek and how the whole community had been looking for me. Rev. Larkin had been the only one who asked me what I was doing. When

I showed him my sketchbook it was like he understood and smoothed everything out with my parents.

"That's so cool," Melody said. "You know, he still zones out when he's drawing."

"Speaking of which," Rev. Larkin said, "what do you have to show me? Certainly there are some new drawings you can share."

We finished up our ice cream and after I checked to make sure it was okay with Melody and Lissa, we took Rev. Larkin up to my room. I showed him my sketch books and then pulled the cover off the painting of Allison. He sat at the foot of my bed and seemed to be lost in the painting for a good five minutes. When he turned away from it, he saw the three of us hugging each other. He stood and came to face us.

"You know, there is no official church or state sponsored unions that include three or more people," he said. "It's too bad. I know you don't have strong faith or a church background, Tony. I don't know your backgrounds at all," he said, looking at Lissa and then Melody. They didn't volunteer any information. He took each of our hands together in his. "Well, just know this. God blesses love and when you love one another, God is there. May God under any guise that you recognize him… or her… bless your love and your lives together."

He smiled at us and left the room. I looked at my lovers and we joined in a kiss. Our own amen.

———◁◆▷———

MELODY AND LISSA were learning first-hand about hot Nebraska summers. They hadn't expected to suffer the heat in heavy blue jeans, but I think they were thankful for them as I led them through the cornfield toward a woodlot nearly half a mile away.

"Knee-high by the Fourth of July" is an old saw, but with fast-growing hybrids, fertilizer, and fair weather, the farmers around here would have been worried if the corn was only up to their knees this week. The sharp bladed leaves of the plants scraped and cut along our jeans and unprotected arms as we made our way through rows of corn that Melody could barely see over. They hadn't believed me when I told them that at night they could lie in a cornfield and listen to it growing. Not until we did it last night.

Then we let the cornfield listen to us.

"Are we there yet?" Melody whined.

In the four days it took us to drive from Boston to Nebraska, Melody had tried out the role of plaintive child. It always fell apart, though, when she finished the statement with, "I'm horny."

"Sweetheart, you've got to think of it like city blocks," I answered, trying my best to sound like a patient parent.

"I don't see any sidewalks out here," Lissa laughed.

"The corn rows are our streets," I said. "There are eight city blocks in a mile. The woods are only half a mile from the road, so just four blocks. It's like walking to Nordstrom's."

"Are we going shopping?" Melody asked brightly.

"No. We're going painting... in one of the most beautiful places in the Midwest," I answered. "And I have a surprise for you when we get there."

In fact, while Mom had the girls occupied for an hour at the barbecue yesterday, I'd stolen away long enough to solidify the plan for this morning. When we passed through the fence-row and into the trees, there was a noticeable change in temperature. We'd all worked up a sweat and the break in the heat was a welcome relief. I knew they were going to want to get naked in the stream soon, and I could hardly wait.

"Just a little way, now," I said, leading them down the worn trail.

"Please don't leave us out here," Lissa said. "I didn't bring any breadcrumbs."

"I wouldn't dream of it, darling," I promised. "Wait. Do you hear it?"

I held up a hand and we stopped to listen, calming our breathing so we could hear the burble of a stream running through the woods. A bobwhite sang at the edge of the woods and a squirrel chattered for a minute then gave up its scolding at our imagined intrusion. I motioned them forward and moments later we came to the edge of the little stream. Spring had been wet in Nebraska, so there was plenty of water in the shallow pool the stream flowed through. Later in the summer, it would barely be a rivulet as everything dried up.

The girls gasped when they saw it, but their eyes were immediately drawn to the rock out in the middle of the narrow basin. On it was perched a vision of loveliness in a halter top and rolled up jeans, her feet gently kicking at the water.

"You can still find it," Beth said.

"You are a goddess," Melody said as she sat on the ground to take her shoes and socks off. Lissa was right beside her. I shed my backpack full of art supplies, but just stood there watching the excited girls roll up their pants legs and wade into the water.

"Try a Grace," I suggested.

"What?" Lissa asked.

I quoted:

"Which of the fairest three
To-day will ride with me?
My steeds are all pawing at the threshold of the
morn:
Which of the fairest three
To-day will ride with me?
Across the gold Autumn's whole Kingdom of
corn?"

As I knew she would, Beth responded.

"I will, I - I – I
young Apollo let me fly
Along with thee,
I will, I - I - I,
The many wonders see
I - I - I – I
And thy lyre shall never have a slacked string
I, I, I, I,
Thro' thy golden day will sing."

"That's beautiful. What is it?" Lissa asked.

"A Verse to Apollo and the Three Graces by John Keats," I answered. "We had to memorize it in high school."

"And you just happened to remember it now?" Lissa chuckled.

"No. We both reviewed it yesterday," I laughed. "I thought this setting with the three of you would be a great place to do my own painting of The Three Graces."

"Ooh. Do we get to be naked in the water?" Melody giggled.

"I hope so," Beth said. "That's the only reason I agreed to do it."

"Hey, wait a minute…" I started.

"Okay. I confess. It's the reason I *suggested* it. If you two are willing, I mean," Beth amended.

"Mmm." Lissa hummed when she'd waded to the rock and given Beth a kiss on the cheek. "My only question is, 'why did you want Melody and me here with you?' You know we're okay with Tony painting you."

Beth was my best friend all through high school. In fact, we'd been friends since first grade. She was a short, plump girl who just happened to be the smartest kid in school. In her speech as valedictorian of our class, she told everyone that we would surprise each other with what we would become.

Well, she certainly surprised me. She'd changed dramatically from when we left for college. She'd shed uncounted pounds and was a real voluptuous dish. The subject, the setting, and the participants were all her idea.

"After I saw that other painting that Tony did—Allison?—I realized that you two were going to be in any painting he did of me. I think she knew you were there when Tony painted her. I just decided to make it explicit. Besides…"

Beth took a deep breath but didn't go on. Melody came up on her other side and kissed her cheek like Lissa had.

"Besides what?"

"Oh, you'll think I'm terrible. Maybe this wasn't such a good idea."

"Dumpling," I said, finally wading into the water myself. I went right up to her and kissed her on the lips so she'd know we were all here and in the open. "You've been my friend for as long as I can remember. Why would you ever imagine I'd think you were terrible?"

Beth reached her finger up and touched her lips where I had. Then she leaned over and softly kissed Melody. When they parted she turned and kissed a smiling Lissa.

"I've been so selfish," she finally went on. "You were so nice to me on the phone and then Sunday night when you got here. I felt so comfy with you at the barbecue yesterday. And I…I…" She hesitated again.

"I-I-I-I, Through thy golden day will sing," I chanted.

"I like seeing naked girls," she burst out. We were shocked silent for a second then all three burst out laughing.

"That makes four of us, I think," I said. "What's wrong with that?"

"But they're your girls and I wasn't thinking pure thoughts," she said, laughter breaking through her own remorse.

Melody and Lissa looked at each other, grinning. In one fluid move, both girls stripped off their t-shirts and stood proudly in front of Beth.

"Happy?" Melody asked. She nudged me and I pulled my shirt off, too.

Now the only one wearing a top, Beth worked her mouth open and closed a couple of times and then unleashed two of the biggest breasts I'd ever seen. She'd lost weight all right, but none of it seemed to come off of her bosom. I was amazed that she could carry around so much weight up top on her tiny five-foot frame and not topple over.

"Wow!" I know I said it, but it sounded like a chorus to me. Melody and Lissa smooshed themselves into Beth in a hug of amazing proportions while I waded out of the stream with the four tops and dropped them on my pack.

"Now that we've got that out of the way," I said, "maybe we can get some posing and sketching done."

Twenty-One

I THOUGHT about talking the girls into losing their jeans, but it was cute the way they were wading in the creek with their pants legs rolled up. They continued to cluster around the rock where Beth sat and I figured that would be as good a setting as any. I got my sketchbook set and then plugged my mp3 player into a tiny speaker I'd seen advertised on late night TV a couple of weeks ago. It filled the clearing with an eerie note of flute music.

"Shakuhachi!" Beth shouted.

"Beautiful. A flute?" Melody asked.

"Japanese Bamboo Flute," I answered. "There's a few cuts of new age flute music, too. I wanted something we could all hear and that wouldn't sound out of place here."

"I expected you to put on your headset," Lissa said. "Are you going to be able to work without closing everything out?"

"It's something I discovered when I drew Allie," I said as I ripped through a couple of warmup sketches. "She wanted to hear the music, too, and it affected the way she posed."

"I'll say," Beth joined in. "I was absolutely knocked out by that painting. I started crying as soon as I saw it."

"Well, remember that I did the painting in isolation, and yes, I was plugged in when I did it. I only did the sketches when we were together. Like today. It's hard to do a good painting in the wild. Someday I'll get the hang of *plein air* painting."

"How do you want us to pose?"

"Beth, stay on the rock, but can you tuck your left leg up under you? The Graces are happy characters—goddesses of charm, beauty, nature, creativity, and um…" I paused. All three girls looked at me questioningly.

"And…?"

"Um… and fertility, I guess." I don't know why that made me embarrassed. But it was so much more intimate-sounding than the other characteristics.

"No big bellies today, okay?" Beth asked. "It took me all year to lose mine."

"Right. Okay, here's who you are. Lissa, you're Aglaea which means 'Splendor.' Beth, you get to be Thalia. That means 'Good Cheer.' And Melody, my bubbly darling, you get to be Euphrosyne, goddess of mirth."

"Wooo!" Melody laughed. She scooped up a bit of water from the creek and flicked it at the other two girls. They jumped and if I hadn't calmed them down, there'd have been a water fight in about two seconds. Fine, but maybe later.

"Wait!" I commanded. "Melody, that's the pose I want. With you leaning in to flick water at the others. But you don't need to do it again until just before I finish. Lissa, turn to look at me a little. Lips apart, a little surprised. Nice. Beth, you're the surprise. Lift your chin. Lean in to Lissa to kiss her cheek. Nice. Nice. Can you hold it?" I quickly snapped a couple of reference photos on my camera.

"I don't mind this," Beth said. I watched as she let her lips glide across Lissa's cheek. Sexy as hell.

"No wonder I'm splashing you two," Melody pouted. "When do I get a kiss?"

"Oh, you beautiful goddess," Beth said. "Anytime you want." She turned quickly out of her pose and put a kiss on the tip of Melody's nose, then snapped back into position.

Hey! Was my best friend putting the make on my girl-friends? Hmm. Did I mind?

It took me all of three seconds to process that information and decide that I didn't mind at all. The three girls chattered about everything from the weather to school to clothing as I sketched and the music filled the woods around us.

One of the characteristics of the classic paintings of the three graces by Rubens and Raphael is that one of them always has her back to the artist. Frankly, my three were all too beautiful to hide. Lissa's unbelievable body has always captivated me, but I could get lost just looking at her face. The way Beth had to stretch up just a little to kiss Lissa tightened and lifted her chest. She developed that chest when she was chubby. Now that the rest of her body was slim, her breasts sagged down a bit when they weren't being supported. But stretching did amazing things and her nipples were surprisingly small and erect, perched on top of the mounds.

I asked Melody to shift in just a little closer, which pushed her right breast into Beth's left. Every once in a while, I could see one or the other of the two girls shift just enough to let their breasts rub together and cause their nipples to stand out even more.

"My feet are getting cold," Lissa said after a while. They'd been standing in the water for about forty-five minutes and I had a pretty good sketch.

"Okay. Melody, now." On command, she dipped her fingers into the water and splashed the other two. I took a quick mental photo of the water and ducked my head to the drawing as the girls' pose broke down into laughter. They each got a good splash at each other before they waded out of the creek.

We'd brought a couple of blankets and spread them out on the ground. The girls dried their feet and flopped out as I put away the sketching materials. When I looked back at them, Lissa was truly kissing Beth as Beth's back arched up pushing a nipple into Melody's mouth. I know how much Melody loves breasts. Her favorite position while we are making love together usually includes having one of Lissa's nipples in her mouth. It was quickly apparent that Beth liked it, too.

"You guys!" Beth said as she broke from the kiss and started to sit up. "I didn't come out here to get all involved with Tony's girlfriends."

"We know. You want Tony," Melody said. "But you're so luscious. I didn't mean to make you uncomfortable."

"That's not it," Beth moaned. "I love it. I mean I *really* love it. Can we just cuddle a little bit? I need to tell you all something."

I stretched out behind Lissa and reached my hand across to Melody so that we were all four connected together.

"Dumpling, you can tell us whatever you want. Now that Mel and Liss are here with me, I'm not quite as uptight as I was when we were alone. I don't know if I can give you what you really want, but we'll all be here for you."

"That's just it, Tony. You were always there for me. That's why I thought I could take advantage of you at the party. I was on a mission."

"That's understandable," Lissa said. "I remember when I went after Jack. He'd protected me and guided me for five years as and I was determined that he was going to be more than my guardian. I was on a mission and he didn't stand a chance." We all laughed.

"Tony and I were never romantically involved," Beth said. "I'm not sure either of us even considered the boy and girl part of our relationship. We were always just friends."

"More than *just* friends," I responded. "We've always been *best* friends."

"Right. Brilliant social outcasts and best friends. But I couldn't wait to get away from here. I was going to reinvent myself. Lose weight. Get a boyfriend. Show all those guys back here what they missed."

"You certainly did that!" I said. "Remember the volleyball game? None of the guys could play worth a damn because they were all looking at you."

"More than anything else, all I wanted to do was snub them," Beth explained. "All but you. I thought... I thought I could use you. I'm sorry."

"Hey, any guy but Tony would have jumped at the chance to jump you," Melody said. "You weren't counting on the fact that we already had our greedy little talons into him."

"That's just it. And I don't think your talons are greedy at all," Beth continued. "I came home thinking I could just kiss Tony and he'd fall back with a hard-on and take my cherry, then I could go back to my girlfriend."

"What?? Your what?" I was knocked out. Beth had a girlfriend? She'd never said anything about that.

"It was no accident that I chose to go to an all-girls college. I already knew who I fantasized about in high school and it wasn't a football player. It really didn't take me long after I got to college to hook up with Barbara. It started with studying together and then long talks instead of studying and then little touches and… well, you get the idea. We were a couple by Halloween."

"You never said anything in all your text messages about a girlfriend," I said. "We must have had a hundred messages a week during September and October."

"But it was getting less and less. Neither of us came home for Thanksgiving and I went straight to Hawaii for my Christmas break. I didn't want anyone here see me before my freshman transformation was complete. Barbara and I worked out and dieted together. I'd started losing weight already during the summer and she kept me on track. But there was always an obstacle between us."

"Let me guess," Lissa said. "I saw these kinds of relationships develop among the models when I was on the road. You thought you were with each other just because you couldn't trust or get a man."

"That's kind of it," Beth admitted. "Specifically, Barbara thought I was only with her because I thought no man would have me. And when I turned out to have a good body and tits that every guy wants to play with, she was afraid that I'd leave her as soon as a guy paid attention to me. So she broke up with me when the term ended."

"Oh, Dumpling! That's terrible," I said. I was close enough that I could stroke her bare back with my right hand and she didn't seem to mind a bit.

"I thought that if I came home and got good old trusty friend Tony to fuck me, then I could go back to school in the fall and tell her that I'd had a boy and now I'm sure I want her. I'm sorry, Tony. I wasn't considering your feelings at all. I wasn't thinking that you might no longer be a virgin. And I wasn't thinking that you might be hurt by me using you like that. I figured, hey, he's never had a girl. We'll fuck and I'll leave, or at worst, we'll have a summer fling and then go our separate ways again. I'm sorry."

There was a shifting of positions. I've never been able to figure out exactly how we do this, even when it's just the three of us. We just slide over each other and suddenly a different person is in the middle. Since none of us had put our shirts back on, the sliding was particularly delicious. Anyway, when it ended up, Melody and I had Beth sandwiched between us, just holding her and Lissa was draped mostly over Melody with her hand wrapped around Beth's bare waist.

I kissed my old friend on the cheek and she turned to capture my lips in a deep and soulful kiss.

"It's still okay," Melody said. "You don't have to do anything you don't want to do. You've been friends with Tony for years and Lissa and I are just catching up. We'll all do anything that friends can do for a friend."

Beth turned those lovely lips on Melody and I could see their hearts accelerating. I swear I was just reaching to feel their heartbeats when I found my hand cupping Beth's breast. She moaned as she turned back to me and glanced down at my hand.

"Tony..."

"If you still want to make love, we can," I said. "But you don't have to. And you don't have to worry about what any of us will think."

"And if you want to make love out here in this beautiful setting, but just want us girls, that's all right, too. Right, Tony?" Lissa said. I nodded.

"Wait. Have sex with the two of you and not with Tony?" Beth asked. "How would that work? I mean, Tony you'd have to…"

"Don't worry," Melody giggled. "*Someone* here would take care of Tony."

———⊲◆▷———

THERE WAS MORE talk. More cuddling. More kissing. More impossible flowing from one position to another. Someplace in the action, we lost the rest of our clothes. Beth was overwhelmed with our loving. She found a blonde head and a redhead each between her legs bringing her to two delicious orgasms. She returned the favors in kind and, while she ate Melody, *my* fingers brought her to another climax. As I lay on my back with Lissa gliding on my cock, Melody held Beth and Beth simply held my balls, feeling them pulse as I came inside my lover.

We rushed back into the creek to wash the sweat off and the girls got into a splashing fest. I scrambled out of the water and took half a dozen quick photos of the three having fun. I began to rework my drawing in my head. Why did everything have to be so classical? The three graces were about fun.

We were dry and pulling our clothes together when Beth came up to me and laid another hot kiss on my lips and tongue. As she did, she stroked my cock and felt it grow in her hand. When I was fully erect—which didn't take long—she gave it a squeeze and broke our kiss.

"I'm not saying never," Beth said as she looked into my eyes. "I'm just not ready now. Thank you for being the best friend on earth."

We hugged each other tightly and soon Melody and Lissa had us sandwiched between them in a group hug. My erection was delightfully pressed against Beth's stomach. We all pulled back to get dressed and Beth took one last look at my cock before I tucked it into my shorts.

"'And thy lyre shall never have a slacked string,'" she quoted. "You know, I never realized what that line meant." We all laughed and headed back down the rows of corn to civilization.

It was time to go home.

THE END

Also by Devon Layne

(Now available as Kindle eBooks.
Print versions coming soon!)

The Model Student Series

Book One: Mural (Now in Paperback!)
Book Two: Rhapsody Suite (Now in Paperback!)
Book Three: Diva (Now in Paperback!)
Book Four: Triptych (Paperback coming soon)
Book Five: Odalisque (Paperback coming soon)
Book Six: The Prodigal (Paperback coming soon)

Erotic Paranormal Romance Western Adventures

Redtail (Now in Paperback)
Blackfeather (Paperback coming in
November, 2016)
Yelloweye (Coming in 2017)

Visit http://DevonLayne.com for more books!